Classic Words

Michael Clay Thompson

Royal Fireworks Press
Unionville, New York

Royal Fireworks   Language Arts   by Michael Clay Thompson

September 2015

Royal Fireworks Press
PO Box 399
41 First Avenue
Unionville, NY 10988-0399
(845) 726-4444
fax: (845) 726-3824
email: mail@rfwp.com
website: rfwp.com

ISBN: 978-0-88092-219-7

Printed and bound in Unionville, New York, on acid-free paper using
vegetable-based inks at the Royal Fireworks facility.

Publisher: Dr. T.M. Kemnitz
Editors: Jennifer Ault and Rachel Semlyen
Cover photo: Dr. T.M. Kemnitz
Book and cover designer: Kerri Ann Ruhl

4jn5   ps

Table of Contents

For my wife,
Myriam Borges Thompson

introduction

What are the best words in the English language? Several years ago I sorted dubiously through recommended word lists and began wondering whether direct study of such vocabulary lists is really worthwhile. Does long-term mastery of vocabulary result from such activities as briefly looking up a word, writing down the definition, and using the word in a sentence, especially if there is no deep exposure to the word as it has been used in literature? How do we learn the nuances of meaning and the subtle possibilities of phrasing that are involved in mastering new words? How many times must we be exposed to a word before it loses its strange otherness and seems familiar? How can we identify the advanced language that is replete in the world of books, in the world of scholarly and professional ideas? How can we find the vocabulary that we really must know if we are to feel comfortable in a world of words? What words are most important to know?

To answer these questions, I began marking the advanced vocabulary in every English language classic I read, and I developed a computer database in which I collected the thousands of vocabulary examples I found. In my computer, I entered the word, the sentence the word was in, the chapter, author, and title. *King Lear* took me 251 entries. Orwell's *1984* took 315 entries. *The Great Gatsby* took 232 entries. Some summers, I typed these words for hours every day. Ten years later, I had collected 21,000 examples of words from seventy-six classics, and at last I have a sample large enough to know, with certainty, that some words are found in most of the best books in English and American literature.

These classic words—words so venerable that they have become classics in themselves—are important to the profound understanding of most good novels, plays, poems, and essays and should be known to all of us as we embark on our journey through good literature.

What are the classic words? Some of the answers may surprise you. Among the most frequently found classic words are *serene, manifest, abate, austere, tangible, palpable, stolid, odious*, and *sagacity*. We also find *morose, inexorable, oblique, billow, ignominy*, and *sallow*. *Alacrity* is there, and *rebuke*, and *zenith*. Would you have expected *maxim* to be common? Or *vestige*? Would you have expected *lurid* to be a classic word?

In this book I discuss some of the most important classic words in the English language, showing how American and British authors have used them. My purpose is to provide a richer exposure to each word than has been otherwise available, and to do so in a way that reveals to readers that each of these words is not only in the classics but is itself a vocabulary classic—a word of such quality that it has been a ubiquitous presence in good English.

1 countenance

Among the most classic of the classic words, the modern English noun *countenance* comes through Middle English and Old French from the Latin verb *continere*, to hold. The countenance is the face, and especially the human contents of the face. In a person's countenance we may see sadness, anger, love, or doubt. We see the person, not just the physiognomy or facial physiology.

The noun *countenance* has been used by Toni Morrison and Eudora Welty, by George Orwell and F. Scott Fitzgerald, by Joseph Heller and Harper Lee, and by toad-maker Kenneth Grahame. Robert Louis Stevenson used it. Harriet Beecher Stowe used it. Swift, Defoe, Milton, and Shakespeare used it. We find *countenance* in *Ethan Frome*, in *Peter Pan*, in *Lord Jim*, and in *The Mayor of Casterbridge*. We find it in Ralph Ellison's *Invisible Man* and in Mary Shelley's *Frankenstein*. We find it in *Jane Eyre*. And in *Ivanhoe*. And in *Walden*. *Countenance* appears in seemingly every book of note in English and American literature for four hundred years.

Countenance is ubiquitous, and it is ubiquitous because it is our best word for the visible self, the individuality that shows in our faces. It is a word of high humanity, and upon reflection we realize that we would have expected human beings writing about human meanings to make use of such a human word.

How is *countenance* used in sentences? Well, in the classics we find a forbidding countenance, a storming countenance, a cheerful countenance, and an ailing countenance. We find a grave countenance and a fearful countenance, a smiling countenance and a martyr's countenance. There is a sad countenance, a sour countenance, a benevolent countenance, and a saturnine countenance. There is a good-natured countenance. Shakespeare described a king's countenance, a countenance surely like a father, and a ghostly countenance "more in sorrow than in anger." King Lear has "that in your countenance which I would fain call master." In *Paradise Lost*, Milton described a countenance filled with "studious thoughts abstruse," a countenance "too severe to be beheld," and a countenance filled with "doubtful hue."

In the eighteenth century, Swift, Defoe, and Mary Wollstonecraft relied on *countenance* for their descriptions. Defoe's Robinson Crusoe found that in Friday, "it was easy to see joy and courage in the fellow's countenance." Defoe described a countenance that "discovered a strange eagerness," a countenance "most inexpressibly dreadful, impossible for words to describe," and a "very good countenance, not a fierce and surly aspect." Robinson spoke to Friday "with a raised voice and cheerful countenance." Jonathan Swift, in the fiercely satirical *Gulliver's Travels*, noted "something in their countenances that made my flesh creep with a horror I cannot express." Gulliver found people "whose countenances and habit expressed so much misery and want," and he quailed when the "fierceness of this creature's countenance all together discomposed me." Mary Wollstonecraft, in her brilliant *Vindication of the Rights of Woman*, objected that in "the countenance of girls we only look for vivacity and bashful modesty." She observed how "mental grace, not noticed by vulgar eyes, often flashes across a rough countenance."

In the nineteenth century, British and American authors used *countenance* in seemingly every description. Jane Austen, in *Pride and Prejudice*, described a pleasant countenance, a good-humoured countenance, a resolute composure of countenance, a steady countenance, an expression of goodness in the countenance, and a countenance of grave reflection. In Mary Shelley's 1816 *Frankenstein*, Shelley noted a wan countenance, frowning and angry countenances, angelic countenances, and a countenance that bespoke bitter anguish. "Oh," she noted, "no mortal could support the horror of that countenance." Washington Irving described a character with "short curly black hair, and a bluff, but not unpleasant countenance."

In 1820 William Wordsworth's Scottish friend Sir Walter Scott wrote that the characters in *Ivanhoe* had a fair and comely countenance, a countenance as pale as death, a countenance that appeared elated, a deep flush of shame that suffused a handsome countenance, and a countenance on which premature age had stamped its ghastly features. "It appeared, indeed," wrote Scott, "from the countenance of this proprietor, that he was of a frank but hasty and choleric temper."

Across the Atlantic, James Fenimore Cooper used *countenance* in *The Last of the Mohicans* to describe the contents of his characters' faces. Cooper found an austere countenance, a dejected countenance, an angry countenance, and a haggard and careworn countenance. He eerily described "that sort of dull unmeaning expression which might be supposed to belong to the countenance of a specter" and noted how "the countenance of Uncas changed from its grave composure to a gleam of intelligence and joy." In the countenances of his characters, Cooper found vacancy, dignity, gravity, and guile.

Emily Brontë's immortal *Wuthering Heights* contains an anguished countenance, a grim countenance, and a perplexed countenance. There is an imploring countenance. Heathcliff's "black countenance looked blightingly through." In the countenances of these characters, we find meditation, shame, pride, trouble, and blankness. We see a countenance grow deadly pale and a countenance from which horror gradually passes. Catherine's countenance had "a wild vindictiveness in its white cheek."

Emily Brontë's sister Charlotte used *countenance* in her 1847 classic *Jane Eyre* to describe "an expression of almost insupportable haughtiness in her bearing and countenance." "I don't know," she wrote, "what sphynx-like expression is forming in your countenance."

In all of his novels, Nathaniel Hawthorne used *countenance* to describe his profoundly drawn characters. He created characters whose countenances were blank, dull, dark, grim, benign, rigid, scornful, glowing, cheery, wan, unreal, pleasant, undismayed, and benevolent. In the 1851 *House of Seven Gables*, Hawthorne wrote that the "aspect of the venerable mansion has always affected me like a human countenance."

Other American writers used *countenance* to describe the physiognomy's visible humanity. Harriet Beecher Stowe noted countenances that were overcast, sad, scowling, and good-natured. Hawthorne's friend Melville created countenances that were composed, glad, benevolent, and curious. Thoreau recalled "Achilles' reproof to Patroclus for his sad countenance." Henry James described how "his pale unlighted countenance had a sort of thin transfiguration." Mark Twain wrote that the "boding uneasiness took possession of every countenance." Stephen Crane noted a morose countenance and described how the "officers were impatient and snappy, their countenances clouded with the tales of misfortune."

Kipling, Conrad, and Stevenson loved *countenance*, and Thomas Hardy used it so often that one could fill pages of examples from his novel alone. In *The Mayor of Casterbridge*, Hardy described a ruddy and fair countenance, a smiling countenance, the statuesque repose in a young girl's countenance, an old woman of mottled countenance, and a martyr's countenance. Like Hawthorne, Hardy applied the word to architecture: "These bridges," he wrote, "had speaking countenances." In *The Return of the Native*, Hardy described "the imperturbable countenance of the heath," and he observed that in Clym Yeobright's face "could be dimly seen the typical countenance of the future." Hardy found a countenance overlaid with legible meanings, a countenance slightly flagging, and a countenance that became crimson.

In the twentieth century, authors continued to use *countenance* to explore the animate dimensions of the face. We find it in Barrie's *Peter Pan* to describe a handsome countenance, a tallow countenance, and a melancholy countenance. Kenneth Grahame used it in *The Wind in the Willows* to describe "the stern unbending look on the countenances of his silent friends." Edith Wharton used it in *Ethan Frome* to describe Ethan's wife's gaunt countenance. Fitzgerald used it in *The Great Gatsby* to describe how "the countenance of a stout old lady beamed down into the room." Nobel Prize-winner Pearl Buck used it in *The Good Earth* to describe how "he had learned now from that impassive square countenance to detect small changes at first invisible to him." George Orwell used it in *Animal Farm* to describe how "Napoleon appeared to change countenance." Ralph Ellison used it in its verbal form in *Invisible Man*: "We will not countenance any aggressive violence." Harper Lee and Toni Morrison used *countenance*, and Eudora Welty described "persons I have seen or noticed or remembered in the flesh—a cast of countenance here, a manner of walking there."

Among modern authors, Joseph Heller, in his brilliant and irreverent *Catch-22*, manifested a fondness for *countenance*. Heller described a storming countenance, a "fierce, regal, just and forbidding countenance," and a spherical countenance. Heller observed the "continuing rainfall, soaking mordantly into each man's ailing countenance like the corrosive blot of some crawling disease."

Though this may seem to have been an elaborate presentation of examples of *countenance*, these have given only a minute indication of the presence of this word in English and American literature. Consider briefly what a complete listing might contain, even if it only included the most famous authors who have written in English.

And what does this inspection of one word reveal that we might not have gained far more easily from a careful glance at a good dictionary? We find, in a way that overwhelms doubt, that *countenance* is an indispensable word, so replete and pervasive in literature that not to know it would be a salient defect in one's command of English. We find that in its manifold usage, it reveals the extraordinary sensitivity of writers who are observing the extraordinary sensitivity of the human face. We find that *countenance* has been an ideal word for extending the human imagination and the human introspection. We find that the uses of *countenance* demonstrate the synthetic genius of the mind and the divergent possibilities of creativity. And perhaps most importantly, we suspect that this word reveals to us our most important subject: ourselves.

2 profound

The English adjective *profound*, one of the English language's great classic words, means deep, very deep. The depth may be physical, as the wine-dark depths of the waving ocean, or it may be human, as the consciousness of intellectual depth, or it may be the emotional depth of a sigh. *Profound* derives from the Latin *pro*, forward, and *fundus*, bottom. Whatever is profound is of, in, or from the bottom. In the archaic past, English speakers used *profound* as a noun—a synonym for *abyss*.

Being a sapient species, *Homo sapiens sapiens* has always had a particular fascination with things profound. Moth-like, we flap toward the deepest light, wanting to know more, wanting to find deep illumination. Being an emotional species, we feel deeply, and we record these feelings in our writing. It should come as no surprise that deep literature is filled with profundities, and we find the word *profound* in English and American literature from Shakespeare's *Hamlet* to Toni Morrison's *Beloved*. Lord Hamlet, we will recall, "raised a sigh so piteous and profound / As it did seem to shatter all his bulk / And end his being." In *Beloved*, "Sethe learned the profound satisfaction Beloved got from storytelling." *Hamlet* was published in 1601, and *Beloved* in 1988—a span of 387 years.

In the meantime, *profound* was used by Milton, Swift, Wollstonecraft, Mary Shelley, Scott, Cooper, the Brontës, Hawthorne, Stowe, Melville, Dickens, James, Twain, Hardy,

Stevenson, Crane, Wells, Conrad, Kipling, Barrie, Joyce, Fitzgerald, Wilder, Faulkner, Steinbeck, Wright, Ellison, Heller, Knowles, Lee, Plath, and Welty. And, of course, by everyone else, too.

What things are described as profound in literature? There are those things one expects: profound ideas, profound silence, profound meaning, and profound sighs. But there are also surprising and creative usages: Sylvia Plath's Esther Greenwood feels "the profound void of an empty stomach." Kipling's *Kim* "salaamed profoundly." And in *Macbeth* there "hangs a vaprous drop profound."

In *Paradise Lost*, a profound poem if ever there was one, Milton described darkness profound, this gloom of Tartarus profound, and the void profound. Milton's Satan, perhaps the inadvertent star of the show, gleams with charismatic malice: "Hail horrors, hail / Infernal world, and thou profoundest Hell / Receive thy new Possessor."

In 1726 Jonathan Swift used *profound* in *Gulliver's Travels* to describe "great wisdom and profound learning," "three profound obeisances," and "profound sleep." Gulliver "was struck with a profound veneration at the sight of Brutus."

Mary Wollstonecraft, in her 1792 *Vindication of the Rights of Woman*, described profound reflection, a profound secret, profound ignorance, and a profound thinker. Her daughter, Mary Shelley, in her 1816 classic *Frankenstein*, used *profound* to describe sleep, study, interest, silence, and feelings. Doctor Victor Frankenstein avers, "I found that I could not compose a female without again devoting several months to profound study and laborious disquisition."

An American novelist who loved to use *profound* was James Fenimore Cooper, who in his 1826 novel *The Last of the Mohicans* described not only the profound silence that we have come to expect but other profundities as well.

We find a character who "dropped his chin to his hand, like a man musing profoundly on the nature of the proposal." Cooper observed that "the fiercest of human passions was already succeeded by the most profound and unequivocal demonstrations of grief." We read that "the woodsman himself, though in his assumed character, was the subject of the solitary being's profoundest reflections."

In his profound novels Nathaniel Hawthorne wrote of profound reverence, profound sleep, profound conclusions, and profound emotion. In *The Scarlet Letter*, Hawthorne described the "profound depth of the minister's repose" and the "profound insight of a seer." In *The House of the Seven Gables*, we find that Hepzibah had "been trying to fathom the profundity and appositeness of this concluding apothegm." It is no wonder that she "returned to her chamber, but did not soon fall asleep, nor then very profoundly."

In Harriet Beecher Stowe's *Uncle Tom's Cabin*, we find profound attention and profound wisdom; we find a character "profoundly studying the figure of the carpet" and another "revolving the matter profoundly in all its phases and bearings." Simeon, we are told, "looked profoundly thoughtful."

In his magnum opus *Moby Dick*, Herman Melville used *profound* profoundly. He not only described "the profound unbounded sea" but also a profound paradox: "Seldom have I known any profound being that had anything to say to this world." Melville noted that "the profound calm which only apparently precedes and prophesies of the storm is perhaps more awful than the storm itself." He described profound homage, profound slumber, profound quiet, profound ignorance, a German emperor who profoundly dines, profound divings, and profound idealized significance. All "truth," Melville observed laconically, "is profound."

Charles Dickens referred to a profound secret in *A Tale of Two Cities*, and Charlotte Brontë found "a source of profound affliction" in *Jane Eyre*. In *Ivanhoe*, one of Scott's characters bows profoundly.

Henry James loved *profound* and used it often. In *The American*, James's characters are profoundly startled, profoundly shocked, and profoundly disagreeable. They meditate profoundly upon music. They have high-breeding and profundity. They feel profound security and wait in profound silence. They react with a profound shrug and are sometimes profoundly unconscious of another's presence. They take profound enjoyment in posture and find something profoundly reassuring in reserve.

Mark Twain described profound distress in *Tom Sawyer*. The "public were profoundly concerned," and there "was a long silence, profound and unbroken." Tom contends with profound sensations and profound loneliness.

Unlike some classic words, *profound* did not recede in the twentieth century but continued as a favorite word of modern authors.

Thomas Hardy, whose works feel modern, used *profound* to describe "the profound sleep which is the result of physical labour." In *The Return of the Native*, "Eustacia's face gradually bent to the hearth in a profound reverie." In *The Mayor of Casterbridge*, characters breathe profoundly.

Robert Louis Stevenson noted the "profound duplicity of life" in *Dr. Jekyll and Mr. Hyde*. Henry Jekyll had made "a discovery so singular and profound" that he could not control it. In his own defense, he noted, "Though so profound a double-dealer, I was in no sense a hypocrite."

Stephen Crane described the profound clamor of war. His youth, Henry Fleming, felt that he "was capable of profound sacrifices, a tremendous death." Looking at the soldiers, he found that their "smudged countenances now expressed a profound dejection."

In H.G. Wells's *The War of the Worlds*, the Martians have landed, and characters find "an oblong profundity with the stardust streaked across it." The scene is eerie: "The farther I penetrated into London, the profounder grew the stillness." In *The Time Machine*, Wells described "such a profound sense of desertion and despair," and his Time Traveller gropes in the profound obscurity.

Joseph Conrad, profound and dubious, is perhaps the prototypical twentieth-century author. Writing in exactly 1900, he used *profound* over and over again in *Lord Jim*. We find profound gasps, profound and calm contemplation of a dying man, and profound and terrifying logic. We find a profound quietude on the face, where there is a profound blackness of the pupils. One character manages "to convey the idea of profound disgust." There is a profound and hopeless fatigue, profound futility, and a moment of real and profound intimacy. Conrad was the master of the disturbing paradox: "he, in his occult way, managed to make his immobility appear profoundly responsive." Conrad described the "sea, blue and profound," "the more profound sombreness in the lustre of the half-transparent dome covering the flat disc of an opaque sea," the "muffled accents of profound grief," and the "purpose of profound meditation." A profound observer, Conrad noted "the amused and profound pity of an old man helpless before a childish disaster." And these are only examples from *Lord Jim*. In *Heart of Darkness*, there is profound stillness, a profound tone, a profound glance, a profound manner, a profoundly pensive attitude, profound serenity, a profound meaning, profound anguish, and of course, profound darkness. In a piercing description, Marlow recalls how "the intimate profundity of that look he gave me when he received his hurt remains to this day in my memory."

Author after author has used *profound*: Kipling's Kim salaamed profoundly. Barrie's Captain Hook was profoundly dejected. In *Ethan Frome*, the "stillness was so profound that he heard a little animal twittering somewhere nearby under the snow." Wilder observed, in *The Bridge of San Luis Rey*, that "even in the most perfect love one person loves less profoundly than the other." "Tom's getting very profound," quips Daisy Buchanan in F. Scott Fitzgerald's *The Great Gatsby*. "He reads deep books with long words in them." In William Faulkner's *As I Lay Dying*, a character "lies on his back, his thin profile in silhouette, ascetic and profound against the sky." In *Of Mice and Men*, there is "a gravity in his manner and a quiet so profound that all talk stopped when he spoke." In George Orwell's chilling and horrible *1984*, Winston Smith "fell asleep murmuring 'Sanity is not statistical,' with the feeling that this remark contained in it a profound wisdom." And in Richard Wright's *Native Son*, his character Bigger Thomas "was alone, profoundly, inescapably."

Ralph Ellison used *profound* in his brilliant *Invisible Man*. Ellison described profound silence, a profound craving for tranquility, and a voice hollow with profound detachment. The Invisible Man "heard the director of Men's House address me with profound respect" and perceived "the beat of profound ideas." There are "eyes that were meant to reveal nothing and to stir profound uncertainty." There are profound sighs, profound distaste, and statements that were "nothing that profound." A character gives a "deeply intoned order, as though each syllable were pregnant with nuances of profoundly important meaning." The Invisible Man gazes at the wall where "an oil portrait of the Founder looked down at me remotely, benign, sad, and in that hot instant, profoundly disillusioned."

In John Knowles's *A Separate Peace*, "it was all profoundly musical to Phineas," and Gene finds that "all my scattered aches found their usual way to a profound seat of pain in my side." In *To Kill a Mockingbird*, Scout Finch precociously observes "my father's profound distaste for the practice of criminal law." Sylvia Plath's Esther Greenwood ironically felt "the same profound thrill it gives me to see trees and grassland waist-high under flood water." "In spite of my profound reservations," Esther reflected, "I thought I would always treasure Joan." Eudora Welty recalls that "My mother couldn't have more profoundly disagreed with that." Joseph Heller's Yossarian, in *Catch-22*, "lived in profound awe and reverence of the majestic, white-haired major with the craggy face and Jehovean bearing." In *Song of Solomon*, Nobel Prize-winner Toni Morrison noted profound similarities and evoked a somehow familiar detachment: "Her mind traveled crooked streets and aimless goat paths, arriving sometimes at profundity, other times at the revelations of a three-year-old."

It is perhaps the most profoundly human aspect of this word that its use is almost entirely metaphorical. To be human, we profoundly see, is to be immersed in depths of all kinds and of many levels. But to perceive these depths in the first place, and then to realize that we have had the intelligence and consciousness to do so—that is a moment of profound self-understanding.

3 manifest

The English word *manifest* comes to English from the Latin *manifestus*, struck by the hand. *Manifest* can be an adjective, a transitive verb, or a noun. It resurfaces as the adverb *manifestly* and the noun *manifestation*. To be manifest is to be evident, to be obvious, like a slap.

From Shakespeare to Toni Morrison, English language authors have used *manifest* to describe obvious and evident things. There are manifest fools, manifest reasons, and manifest clues. There are manifest sentiments. In Shakespeare's 1606 *King Lear*, there were "heinous, manifest, and many treasons," to put it mildly.

In 1667 Milton used *manifest* with theological elegance: "The Son of God renders praises to his Father for the manifestation of gracious purpose towards Man."

In *Gulliver's Travels*, Jonathan Swift's gullible Gulliver observes that "it was manifest I had neither the strength or agility of a common Yahoo." Gulliver describes "causes manifestly known to be unjust, vexatious, or oppressive" and worries about one "so wrapped up in cogitation that he is in manifest danger of falling down every precipice." He observes that he "had lived several years, as it was manifested from my beard."

In 1816 Mary Shelley pitied her poor *Frankenstein* monster for "the loathing and scorn which his protectors had manifested towards him," and Victor Frankenstein "manifested the greatest eagerness to be upon deck" where he could scan the ice for sight of his quilted monster.

Walter Scott used *manifest* in his great *Ivanhoe*, where a knight in shining armor "had manifested himself, on many occasions, a brave and determined soldier." For one character, Scott observed "the passive and indifferent conduct which he had manifested on the former part of the day." *Ivanhoe's* female characters, we should note, manifest modern qualities of strength and independence, making this book generations ahead of its time.

In 1826, one hundred years after Swift's 1726 *Gulliver's Travels*, James Fenimore Cooper used *manifest* in *The Last of the Mohicans* to describe, well, everything. "There was at first a fierce and manifest display of joy," Cooper wrote, "and then it was instantly subdued in a look of cunning coldness." Cooper described how a character's "grave countenance manifested no opinion of his own superiority" and how another "washing off the stain, was content to manifest, in this simple manner, the slightness of the injury." In *The Last of the Mohicans*, characters manifest indifference, anger, and impatience. They manifest alarm. In one instance, "Munro witnessed this movement with manifest uneasiness, nor did he fail to demand an instant explanation." Milton would have been pleased to see Cooper describe "the power of the Lord so manifest in this howling wilderness." Cooper described how the struggles of the spirit are "manifested in frequent and heavy sighs" and how "manifestations of weakness were exhibited by the young and vain of the party." At one point, the characters are enjoined to "Manifest no distrust, or you may invite the danger you appear to apprehend."

When Cooper wrote of these manifest dangers and manifest emotions in the howling wilderness of North America, Emily Brontë was eight years old, growing up with her brilliant siblings across the stormy Atlantic. In 1847, four years before Cooper's death, she would write her immortal

Wuthering Heights and describe "Hindley's manifestations of scorn" for Heathcliff. Brontë described "an aversion to showy displays of feeling—to manifestations of mutual kindliness" and portrayed the indifference of the world with clear simplicity: "even the gate over which he leant manifested no sympathizing movement to the words."

The same year, Emily's sister Charlotte used *manifest* in *Jane Eyre* to describe "words in which the sentiment was manifested," to note that something can be "very unobtrusive in its manifestations," and to observe "a universal manifestation of discontent."

Nathaniel Hawthorne loved *manifest*, and he used it in all of his works, especially to explore the subtle ways in which the hidden is revealed. In *The Scarlet Letter*, Hawthorne described many hidden things that were manifest: forbidden sympathy, an unspoken crime, and Heaven's dreadful judgment, for three examples. Hawthorne described how the "very ideal of ignominy was embodied and made manifest in this contrivance of wood and iron" and how things "become manifest by unmistakable tokens." With Chillingworth, Hawthorne ironically observed "the strong interest which the physician ever manifested in the young clergyman."

In *The House of the Seven Gables*, Hawthorne found that "God will make it manifest!" He described "Phoebe, whose fresh and maidenly figure was both sunshine and flowers— their essence, in a prettier and more agreeable mode of manifestation." In *The House of the Seven Gables*, "a look of surprise was manifest," and "a certain quality of nervousness had become more or less manifest." Hawthorne's characters try to conceal their feelings: "Not that he could ever be said to converse with her, or often manifest, in any other, very definite mode, his sense of a charm in her society." They conceal their attractions: "Its manifestations were so various, and agreed so little with one another, that the girl knew not what to make of it."

Hawthorne's friend Melville also used *manifest* in his ponderous whale of a story *Moby Dick*, where the monomaniac Ahab "manifested the gloomiest reserve." Melville's unique sentences often demonstrate not only a mastery of words as they are commonly used but a clear originality and independent genius: Melville described that "certain sultanism of his brain, which had otherwise in a good degree remained unmanifested."

While Melville was searching for a whale in an ocean, the eccentric American genius Henry David Thoreau went to the woods and built himself a cabin. He had in mind a "house whose inside is as open and manifest as a bird's nest." Thoreau observed that "the squirrels manifest no concern whether the woods will bear chestnuts this year or not," and he stoically deplored "the accidental possession of wealth, and its manifestation in dress and equipage alone."

In 1859 Charles Dickens used *manifest* in *A Tale of Two Cities* to indicate manifest constraint and a noisome flavor that "becomes manifest in all such places." Dickens noticed that something had done "a world of good which never became manifest," but of course, as Hamlet saw, the good that men do is oft interred with their bones, while the evil lives after them.

In *Silas Marner*, George Eliot described manifestations of regard and caught one character trying to "justify his insincerity by manifesting its prudence." Eliot wrote *Silas Marner* in 1861, as cannons roared to life across the North American continent and the good of many men was interred with their bones.

Henry James published *The American* in 1876. His character Newman (get it?), "now that his prize was gained, felt a peculiar desire that his triumph should be manifest." James described manifestations of ardour and pitied his character, who "took no interest in chatting about his affairs and manifested no desire to look over his accounts." Shocking!—deny us anything, but let us at those accounts. With originality, James described how Newman "wished to make some answering manifestations."

The same year that *The American* appeared, another book was published that was to have a greater and more enduring impact on American literature. In this book, "gradually sounds multiplied and life manifested itself." Furthermore, "the tittering continued; it even manifestly increased." In fact, "he had the manifest sympathy of the house," and there was "tolerably manifest pride in the remembrance." In this book, "her human curiosity presently began to manifest itself by hardly perceptible signs." This book, Mark Twain's *Tom Sawyer*, would eventually evolve into the colloquial and local *Huckleberry Finn* and change the course of American fiction forever. "You don't know me," Huck would aver in his opening salvo of solecisms, "without you have read a book called *Tom Sawyer*." And yup, we don't know nothin' without we have.

Thomas Hardy used *manifest* in *The Mayor of Casterbridge*: "The reason of its unpopularity was soon made manifest," and again in *The Return of the Native*: "One reason for the permanence of the blaze was now manifest." Hardy described how "At every new attempt to look about him the same morbid sensibility to light was manifested."

In *The Time Machine*, H.G. Wells's gifted Time Traveller "could follow up the new-found clue in what was manifestly the proper way."

In Conrad's 1900 novel *Lord Jim*, "The man was a manifest fool." Conrad's characters move in an atmosphere redolent of strangeness: "He followed me as manageable as a little child...with no sort of manifestation," and "Had he been capable of picturesque manifestations he would have shuddered at the thought."

Kipling's Kim coolly observes that "It is manifest that from time to time I shall acquire merit."

In Jack London's *The Call of the Wild*, three doomed travelers are thanked for their hubris by plunging to their deaths through the thawing ice of a frozen river. London noted that "Both men were manifestly out of place," and "Mercedes screamed, cried, laughed and manifested the chaotic abandonment of hysteria." A more intelligent character than these, the dog, Buck, fought his way to survival and wild freedom. At one point, "To Buck's surprise these dogs manifested no jealously toward him."

In George Orwell's 1945 *Animal Farm*, the pigs "were manifestly cleverer than the other animals."

With one eye on Salem and the other on Joe McCarthy, Arthur Miller found that the "witch-hunt was a perverse manifestation of the panic which set in among all classes" in *The Crucible*. The hunted witch "swears that she never saw familiar spirits, apparitions, nor any manifest of the Devil," but the hunters are not deceived; "When the diabolism rises, however, actions are the least important manifests of the true nature of a man."

In *Catch-22*, Joseph Heller described the "lovely, satisfying, maddening manifestations of the miraculous." And in *Song of Solomon*, Toni Morrison observed that "the manifestation it took was a source of great interest to them."

The importance of this word, though perhaps imperceptible at first, has, through examples from four centuries of classic literature, become manifest; life is a foreground and a background, a visible and an invisible, a veil of things manifest and subtle. For those things that strike our perceptions with clarity and force, English-speaking people and their greatest authors use the word that means, literally, struck by the hand: *manifest*.

4 serene

The English adjective *serene* is a descendant of the Greek *xeros*, dry, but the meaning of *serene* is clear, bright, unclouded, calm, tranquil. Well, a dry sky *is* clear and unclouded, but we often see *serene* modifying nouns other than *sky*. In the classics, we find a serene countenance and a serene conscience, serene joy and serene eyes, a serene smile and a serene walk. And of course, we see serene skies and serene waters. In good literature, with its myriad perturbations, it is not surprising to find the presence of a serenity or two to make reading bearable!

Serene has a venerable heritage. More than three hundred years ago in 1667, Milton used *serene* in *Paradise Lost* to describe a serene look, an Angel serene, and "those looks / That wont to be more cheerful and serene / Than when fair morning first smiles on the world." Milton described how "the Son with calm aspect and clear / Light'ning Divine, ineffable, serene, / Made answer."

Fifty-two years later in 1719, Daniel Defoe described serene weather in *Robinson Crusoe* and described how a man "is kept serene and calm by having the events of things hid from his eyes." Of course, just knowing that events are hid from one's eyes can ruffle one's serenity a mite.

In *Pride and Prejudice*, the brilliant Jane Austen described "the serenity of a mind at ease with itself," the "serenity of your sister's countenance," and the happy fact that "Mrs. Bennet was restored to her usual querulous serenity." We are pleased for Mrs. Bennet, to be sure, but we wonder in what particulars of countenance the serenity of a mind at ease with itself would be manifested.

Mary Shelley's 1816 *Frankenstein* is filled with serenities. There is a "calm and serene joy," a "serenity of conscience," an evening that "was warm and serene," and a poor, poor monster who longed to be human: "their feelings were serene and peaceful, while mine became every day more tumultuous." The sensitive, Wordsworthian monster thrilled with romantic raptures toward nature: "A serene sky and verdant fields filled me with ecstasy." The monster-maker, Victor Frankenstein, was something less at peace: "The sky was serene; and, as I was unable to rest, I resolved to visit the spot where my poor William had been murdered."

In Washington Irving's *The Legend of Sleepy Hollow*, the "sky was clear and serene, and nature wore that rich and golden livery which we always associate with the idea of abundance." Well, almost always.

James Fenimore Cooper used *serene* in *The Last of the Mohicans*, where "Throughout the whole of these trying moments, Uncas had alone preserved his serenity."

Jane Eyre, Charlotte Brontë's independent hero, says laconically to Mr. Rochester, "The night is serene, sir." Not so serene, if she knew the secret in the attic.

In *The Scarlet Letter*, Nathaniel Hawthorne described "serene deportment," but Hawthorne's friend Herman did much more than that. Melville described "the serene weather of the tropics" and the way "that serene ocean rolled eastwards from me a thousands leagues of blue." Melville's characters experience "serene household joy" and "the serene tranquilities of the tropical sea," and one is seen "entirely at his ease; preserving the utmost serenity." As the good ship *Pequod* is "under indolent sail, and gliding so serenely along," Ahab, Melville's tormented monomaniac, utters in despair, "What business have I with this pipe? This thing that is meant for sereneness, to send up mild white vapors among mild white hairs." In the end, Ahab and his crew are in for a soaking, and their fate is marked by "the contrasting serenity of the weather, in which, beneath all its blue blandness, some thought there lurked a devilish charm."

Melville described, with eerie, sibilant consonance, "one serene and moonlight night, when all the waves rolled by like scrolls of silver; and by their soft, suffusing seethings, made what seemed a silvery silence, not a solitude." In the end, nature was indifferent to the fate of the mariners: "they swam out of the white curds of the whale's direful wrath into the serene, exasperating sunlight, that smiled on, as if at a birth or a bridal."

In 1854 Henry David Thoreau serenely published his *Walden*, sawn from native American hardwords. Thoreau observed that "my serenity is rippled but not ruffled" and described the "serene and celestial atmosphere," the "vision of serenity and purity," and "open and serene eyes." Thoreau imagined a "bluerobed man, whose fittest roof is the overhanging sky which reflects his serenity." In 1854 an American writer could still write such idealistic words; seven years later the serenity of optimism would be shattered, and the men of Massachusetts would shoulder arms to march south, where Shiloh was waiting for them.

Henry James loved to use *serene*. In *The American*, James described the artistic ignorance of the Philistine: "he might sometimes have been seen gazing with culpable serenity at inferior productions," the tranquility of self-confidence: "She was monumentally stout and imperturbably serene," and the internal peace of aristocracy: "M. de Bellegarde's good wishes seemed to descend out of the white expanse of his sublime serenity with the soft scattered movement of a shower of snow-flakes." James found "wisdom sound, serene, well-directed," and he noted the "soft, serene assurance of a person who, as a duchess, was certain of being listened to."

In *Tom Sawyer*, Mark Twain delightfully described how Tom and Huck "got out their pipes and went serenely puffing around." With merciless perspicacity, Twain observed "a stony-hearted liar reel off his serene statement."

The protomodern novelist for a while, Thomas Hardy discovered "Yeobright preaching to the Egdon eremites that they might rise to a serene comprehensiveness without going through the process of enriching themselves." Sounds like something a returning native would say.

In *The Mayor of Casterbridge*, Hardy described "serene Minerva-eyes" and admired how "the man had risen to serenity." But what would such a man sink to?

One of the horrifying *serene* sentences comes to us from the precocious Stephen Crane, who described civil war: "With serene regularity, as if controlled by a schedule, bullets buffed into men."

H.G. Wells observed the serenity of the sky in *The Time Machine*, and in *The War of the Worlds* he described how "the Martian, without using his Heat-Ray, walked serenely over their guns." As Melville had been, Wells was troubled by the absurd contrast between natural beauty and human misery: "But the trouble was the blank incongruity of this serenity and the swift death flying yonder." (We are reminded of Macduff's existential horror on learning of the slaughter of his innocent wife and babies: "Did Heaven look on and would not take their part?") Wells described "that serene confidence in the future which is the most fruitful source of decadence," and he felt the chill of irony in the air: "That night was a beautiful serenity: save for one planet, the moon seemed to have the sky to herself."

Joseph Conrad's moonrise was different. In *Lord Jim*, Conrad described how the moon "seemed to gloat serenely over the spectacle." Conrad described "Below us the plain of the sea, of a serene and intense blue."

How often the peacefulness of *serene* connotes evil, connotes a disturbing peacefulness where there should be none, connotes a monster at ease with himself! In *Heart of Darkness*, Conrad described how Kurtz "leaned back, serene, with that peculiar smile of his sealing the unexpressed depths of his meanness." Marlowe told his story as the "day was ending in a serenity of still and exquisite brilliance," but soon "the serenity became less brilliant but more profound." Like the meaning, we presume.

Kipling's Kim "puffed serenely," was "serenely prepared for anything," and watched a policeman serenely picking his teeth.

Kenneth Grahame's moon floats over Ratty, Mole, and Badger—and the incorrigible Toad—but with none of the insidious malevolence that we found in the moons of Wells and Melville. Above the wind in the willows, Grahame saw "the moon, serene and detached in a cloudless sky."

James Joyce used *serene* in his 1916 *Portrait of the Artist as a Young Man*, who is seen "leaving his mind serene and dutiful towards her again."

Thornton Wilder described the serene ocean in *The Bridge of San Luis Rey*: "Blurred and streaked became her view of the serene Pacific."

Some of the best uses of *serene* in modern literature come from Ralph Ellison's 1952 masterpiece *Invisible Man*. The invisible man—invisible to the blank, dead eyes of discrimination—feels "as though I had held my breath continuously for an hour under the terrifying serenity that comes from days of intense hunger." In the city, the "sound floats over all, clear like the night, liquid, serene, and lonely."

Above the street, we see "each light serene in its cage of shadows." And the characters are aloof, "too serene and too far away."

In *Catch-22*, Joseph Heller's madcap "Yossarian continued staring in tormented fascination at Aarfy's spherical countenance beaming at him so serenely and vacantly."

John Knowles used *serene* in *A Separate Peace* to describe how "Phineas just walked serenely on, or rather flowed on." With beautiful insight, Knowles wrote of "the serene order of Haydn." In *To Kill a Mockingbird*, Harper Lee observed, "so serene was Judge Taylor's court." Sylvia Plath coolly noted how a "serene, almost religious smile lit up the woman's face." And Nobel Laureate Toni Morrison, in *Beloved*, wrote that "Eighty-six days and his hands were still, waiting serenely each rat-rustling night for 'Hiiii!' at dawn."

Serene, like many words used beautifully by writers, begins at a literal level to describe the peace of a dry, clear sky and ascends to a metaphorical level to compare such a bright and unclouded heaven to the clear, unclouded look of a peaceful face, a peaceful heart, or even the undisturbed, azure tranquility of a peaceful cruelty. Repeatedly, writers have focused on the absurd serenity of nature in the presence of human distress.

5 sublime

If the English adjective *sublime* means noble or majestic (and it does), then why does it contain the Latin stem *sub*, which means under? Well, in Rome, honored objects were placed up on or under (*sub*) the mantel (*limen*) where they could be seen, and so *sublime* means not down but up, up under the mantel, up *sub* the *limen*. As many words do, *sublime* has a number of possible meanings, but they all connote a high, lofty state. *Sublime* may mean exalted, or inspiring, or grand. It may mean outstanding or supreme. Sometimes we use the word as a noun and refer to the sublime.

Sublime has been an important word in English literature for more than three centuries. The sublime poet John Milton used *sublime* in his 1667 masterpiece *Paradise Lost*. Milton's Satan flew through the Air sublime: "and Satan there / Coasting the wall of Heav'n on this side Night / In the dun Air sublime." In *Paradise Lost*, there is a "celestial colloquy sublime," and characters are "Sublime with expectation when to see / In Triumph issuing forth their glorious Chief."

In *Gulliver's Travels*, Jonathan Swift's satirical attack on the stupidity of English society and government, Gulliver appears before the diminutive Lilliputian ruler, "His most sublime Majesty." Gulliver finds ideas that can "be comprehended only by a few persons of sublime genius" and meets characters that must be "treated with the utmost respect due to their sublime dignity."

In 1792 Mary Wollstonecraft used *sublime* in her perspicuous and prescient classic *Vindication of the Rights of Woman*. Of God, she asked, "Why should He lead us from love of ourselves to the sublime emotions?" She considered the future to be one of "a boundless prospect and sublime hopes." She observed that "Gentleness of manners, forbearance and long suffering are such amiable Godlike qualities, that in sublime poetic strains the Deity has been invested with them." For those insensitive to the rights of women, she wished to "give them the salutary sublime curb of principle," and she wished that society would adhere to a "sublime precept" in its treatment of women. Wollstonecraft argued for a "wisdom sublime" and reasoned that "Friendship is a serious affection; the most sublime of all affections, because it is founded on principle, and cemented by time." She discussed "the sublimest virtues," "the language of sublime poetry," "that sublime tenderness, so near akin to devotion," and the "sublime gloom of tender melancholy."

In *Frankenstein*, Mary Wollstonecraft's daughter, Mary Wollstonecraft Shelley, used *sublime* in the romantic horror novel that she crafted with the encouragement of her husband, Percy Shelley, and their friend, George Gordon, Lord Byron. She described "the majestic and wondrous scenes which surrounded our Swiss home—the sublime shapes of the mountains." Over and over, Shelley used *sublime* to describe scenery: "it was augmented and rendered sublime by the mighty alps," and "This valley is more wonderful and sublime, but not so beautiful and picturesque," and "These sublime and magnificent scenes afforded me the greatest consolation that I was capable of receiving." Deep emotions, for a monster. Shelley's patched monster, an autodidact if there was one, turned himself to "the study of what is excellent and sublime in the productions of man," which "filled me with a sublime ecstasy, that gave wings to the soul, and allowed it to soar from the obscure world to light and joy."

But he became a bitter monster in the end: "I cannot believe that I am the same creature whose thoughts were once filled with sublime and transcendent visions of the beauty and majesty of goodness." Well, being stoned by villagers would irritate the best of us.

Sir Walter Scott described the "thrilling sense of the sublime" in *Ivanhoe*, and Charlotte Brontë referred to a "sublime conclusion" and "noble cares and sublime results" in *Jane Eyre*.

One of the authors who used *sublime* most often was Harriet Beecher Stowe in her disturbing 1851 classic *Uncle Tom's Cabin*. Writing with intense incendiary purpose, Stowe succeeded in electrifying the sense of antislavery outrage in millions of Americans. Only a few years after the publication of her novel, that outrage assumed the form of civil war. Abraham Lincoln is supposed to have met Stowe and said, "So you're the little lady who started this big war"; the incident may be apocryphal. But even today, to read her novel is to be shocked, to be stupefied and incredulous at the horror of human slavery. Stowe described a "sublime mystery," mud that was "of unfathomable and sublime depth," "sublime heroism," and a character who "smoked on in sublime tranquility." "How sublimely he had sat with his hands in his pockets," she wrote. She noted that "Sublime is the dominion of the mind over the body," and with a touch of irony she described the "heels of his muddy boots reposing sublimely on the mantelpiece." For slaves there were "no such sublime words of hope," and the "sublime doctrine of love and forgiveness" seemed remote indeed. In *Uncle Tom's Cabin*, "a fellow can't get himself up to any very sublime moral flights." And in death, "that mysterious and sublime change passed over his face, that told the approach of other worlds." The injustice of slavery clarified philosophical ideas: "What a sublime conception is that of a last judgment!"

In 1851, the same year that *Uncle Tom's Cabin* came out, a younger author published another novel, and it was a masterpiece—perhaps the best novel ever written by an American. Herman Melville's *Moby Dick* used the undulating backdrop of the sea to reveal the nightmare of the mind, and his monomaniacal zealot, Ahab, sailed into the literary consciousness of the world. In Melville's monster novel, for that is what it is, there are none of Shelley's sublime landscapes or Stowe's sublime heroisms; Melville's is the ironic zone, where clarities are muted and ambiguous half-truths are partially disclosed. Melville described a "sort of indefinite, half-attained, unimaginable sublimity," where there is "something almost sublime in it." Melville's sublime is rendered mundane, at best, when a character "through his dilated nostrils snuffed in the sublime life of the worlds." "For the most part, in this tropic whaling life," Melville wrote, "a sublime uneventfulness invests you; you hear no news; read no gazettes." When Melville described "whatever is sweet, and honorable, and sublime," it was likely to be with a twist, as in a description of a face: Melville described "the full front of his head. This aspect is sublime"; it is the head of a sperm whale. In fact, Melville returned again and again to this theme, the "considerations touching the great inherent dignity and sublimity of the Sperm Whale."

In *A Tale of Two Cities*, Charles Dickens wondered about things that "sublime intelligences may read in the feeble shining of this earth." And in Henry James's *The American*, "M. de Bellegarde's good wishes seemed to descend out of the white expanse of his sublime serenity with the soft scattered movement of a shower of snow-flakes." Only a frustrated poet, perhaps, would compare sublime serenity to soft scattered snow; how often, in great prose, we are bushwhacked by poetry, ambushed by alliteration.

Mark Twain described "the sublimity of his language" in *Tom Sawyer*.

Thomas Hardy used *sublime* in all of his novels. In *The Return of the Native*, Hardy almost revives Mary Shelley's sublime landscapes. Almost; they are now chastened: "The time seems near...when the chastened sublimity of a moor, a sea, or a mountain will be all of nature that is absolutely in keeping with the moods of the more thinking among mankind." Hardy even used *sublime* to summarize Dante: "Then the whole black phenomenon beneath represented Limbo as viewed from the brink by the sublime Florentine in his vision."

With a wink, Stephen Crane described the youthfulness of youth, marching with callow immaturity on their way to death, not dusty but red: "One was marching with an air imitative of some sublime drum major." In the sacrifice required by war, Crane found "a temporary but sublime absence of selfishness."

By the twentieth century the use of *sublime* seemed to have decreased, but the word maintained a meaningful presence. Kipling's Kim looked for the "fulfillment of sublime prophecy." And in Barrie's *Peter Pan*, the villainous Pirate Smee offered to spare Wendy's life if she would be his mother. She just said no, a decision that would not compromise the authenticity of "our sublime faith in a mother's love." James Joyce looked to "distinguish between the beautiful and the sublime" in his *Portrait of the Artist as a Young Man*. Ralph Ellison's Invisible Man wondered whether she was "calling me beautiful or boogieful, beautiful or sublime." In Arthur Miller's *The Crucible*, "Cheever waits placidly, the sublime official, dutiful." And in Joseph Heller's *Catch-22*, "Aarfy's joy was sublime."

What do we learn from these beautiful sentences, which fall to us from three centuries of writing? Among other things, we see the creative intelligence of wonderful writers, who find new and surprising ways to use words. Perhaps most of us could use *sublime* to describe purple mountains' majesty, but Harriet Beecher Stowe described mud that was of "an unfathomable and sublime depth." Mud. And what, exactly, did Melville mean by describing the front of the sperm whale's head as sublime? And why did Hardy describe the sublimity of the moor as chastened?

Aristotle identified the use of metaphor as one of the clearest signs of high intelligence; this same ability is involved in the superb use of words that we see in great writers. They take these words to new places, applying them in unintended and unexpected ways that fill language with life.

6 prodigious

Our English adjective *prodigious* is the modifying form of the common noun *prodigy*, a combination of *pro*, before, and *agium*, a thing said (think of *adage*). A prodigy, in the ancient meaning, is a foretelling, a pro-adage; it is a phenomenon so extraordinary that it seems an omen. In modern meanings, a prodigy is something wondrous, such as a child prodigy who dazzles adults with displays of genius. In the adjective form, *prodigious* means amazing, or even extraordinarily powerful or large. The essence of all these meanings, though, is the effect on the mind; what is prodigious fills us with astonishment.

Four hundred years ago, *prodigious* was already a strong and viable word in English. In 1594 Shakespeare used *prodigy* in *The Taming of the Shrew* to describe astonished faces, "As if they saw some wondrous moment, / Some comet, or unusual prodigy." Two years later, he used it in *Romeo and Juliet*: "Prodigious birth of love it is to me / That I must love a loathed enemy."

Milton used prodigious in his 1667 *Paradise Lost* to describe "prodigious Births of body or mind," "a Bridge / Of length prodigious joining to the Wall / Immovable," "Satan, who that day / Prodigious power had shown," and "excessive grown / Prodigious motion."

Daniel Defoe loved to use *prodigious*. In his 1719 timeless classic of a problem-solving Englishman marooned on a desert island, *Robinson Crusoe*, Defoe found a prodigious multitude, a prodigious quantity, a prodigy of nature, and a prodigious deal of pains. There were "prodigious numbers of tigers, lions, leopards, and other furious creatures," and Robinson lamented the "prodigious deal of time and labor which it took me up to make a plank or board." Most work, in fact, "required a prodigious time to do alone and by hand." Well, it doesn't take being marooned in the Pacific to teach us that many of life's tasks are prodigious; perhaps that is why we continue to identify with Robinson and appreciate his situation.

In 1726 Jonathan Swift made *prodigious* one of the feature words of his satirical weapon *Gulliver's Travels*. Everywhere Gulliver traveled, he met with the prodigious. There were prodigious birds in the air, prodigious estates, a prodigious defect of policy, and prodigious abilities of mind. Severed "veins and arteries spouted up such a prodigious quantity of blood." Gulliver witnessed prodigious speed, the "bulk of so prodigious a person," and a prodigious plate of steel. The Lilliputians were shocked by Gulliver's prodigious strength. Gulliver found prodigious pots and kettles, a prodigious race of mortals, and a prodigious vessel. He saw a creature with "a girdle about his waist made of the hide of some prodigious animal."

In Jane Austen's *Pride and Prejudice*, "Mr. Darcy is uncommonly kind to Mr. Bingley, and takes a prodigious deal of care of him." Austen's characters can be "prodigiously proud" and can say of others, "I like them prodigiously"—a lovely and generous wording difficult to imagine in our century, though we like it prodigiously.

James Fenimore Cooper, in his 1826 *The Last of the Mohicans*, wrote that "they redoubled efforts that before had seemed prodigious" and beheld "a prodigy of rashness and skill."

Nathaniel Hawthorne used *prodigious* frequently in his dark 1851 classic *The House of the Seven Gables*. Hawthorne described prodigious frowns, a prodigious hurry, a fat woman making prodigious speed, and, wittily, "the prodigious trampling of crow's feet about my temples!" In the dawning morning, Hawthorne wrote, "there was a prodigious cackling and gratulation of Chanticleer and all his family." Few of us, these days, hear the gratulation of Chanticleer.

In the prodigious *Moby Dick*, Herman Melville found prodigious magnitude, a prodigious commotion, a prodigious hurry, a prodigious bed, and a prodigious blood-dripping mass. "With a prodigious noise," Melville wrote, "the door flew open." Melville's character Ishmael described the "prodigious long horn of the Narwhale" and explained how in "another plate [of a book], the prodigious blunder is made of representing the whale with perpendicular flukes." Egad. At sea the "prodigious strain upon the main-sail had parted the weathersheet," and a "boat looks as if it were pulling off with a prodigious great wedding-cake to present to the whales." Unpleasantly, Melville described "one of those problematical whales that seem to dry up and die with a sort of prodigious dyspepsia, or indigestion."

Harriet Beecher Stowe described being amused prodigiously, Charles Dickens referred to prodigious strength, and Henry James observed his character "looking at her prints and photographs (which he thought prodigiously pretty)."

Mark Twain enjoyed using *prodigious* in his post-Civil War classic *Tom Sawyer*. Twain described how the "middle-aged man turned out to be a prodigious personage—no less than the county judge." In *Tom Sawyer*, there is "a chance to deliver a Bible prize and exhibit a prodigy." And gloriously for Tom and Huck, "Each lad had an income, now, that was simply prodigious—a dollar for every weekday in the year and half of the Sundays."

In Robert Louis Stevenson's yohoho and a lot of fun *Treasure Island*, Long John Silver is a prodigious villain and a gifted one. We read that the "Spaniards were so prodigiously afraid" of the pirates, and we listen in as young Jim Hawkins is entrusted with responsibility beyond his years: "Hawkins, I put prodigious faith in you."

In *Dr. Jekyll and Mr. Hyde*, Stevenson wrote that "your sight shall be blasted by a prodigy to stagger the unbelief of Satan."

In *The Red Badge of Courage*, Stephen Crane described "this prodigious uproar" of battle. In *The Time Machine*, H.G. Wells described how the Time Traveller "was still traveling with prodigious velocity." And in *Kim*, Rudyard Kipling described the outcry of the lama, "snuffing prodigiously in his excitement."

Joseph Conrad, in *Lord Jim*, wrote that "Their escape would trouble me as a prodigiously inexplicable event," but in *Heart of Darkness*, he turned more sinister: "It made me hold my breath in expectation of hearing the wilderness burst into a prodigious peal of laughter."

In the soul-searching *A Portrait of the Artist as a Young Man*, James Joyce fearfully described how "The brimstone too which burns there in such prodigious quantity fills all hell with its intolerable stench." Brimstone being sulfur, we can believe that the stench would be intolerable.

Among modern writers, Henry Miller stands out as one who made strong use of *prodigious*. In Miller's strike against government scapegoating, *The Crucible*, we read that there is "a prodigious fear of this court in the country" and that there is "a prodigious stench in this place." Goody Nurse is admonished, "That is a notorious sign of witchcraft afoot,

Goody Nurse, a prodigious sign!" And we learn that there is "a prodigious danger in the seeking of loose spirits."

In Joseph Heller's 1955 anti-novel *Catch-22*, "Major Major grew despondent as he watched simple communications swell prodigiously into huge manuscripts," and one character "launched himself forward in a prodigious dive that crushed the three combatants to the ground beneath him."

And in John Knowles's *A Separate Peace*, there is a fateful tree overhanging a river, and from a high branch of this tree, "you could by a prodigious effort jump far enough out into the river for safety." Unless, of course, you were pushed.

In reading these expressive sentences, we gradually become more aware of the essence of this adjective, *prodigious*, and experience some of its flavor. What, for instance, is the difference between being in a hurry, being in a great hurry, and being in a prodigious hurry? Both Melville and Hawthorne described hurries as prodigious, but why? The difference is in degree and in the effect upon observers. We often see someone in a hurry, or even in a great hurry. These are common and are not prodigious. But when we see someone hurrying in a way that surprises us, that surprises us with disbelief, that makes us want to laugh or cry out, then the hurry is not just great, it is prodigious. Prodigious phenomena are beyond our expectations; they overwhelm our capacity to absorb them.

The prodigious dyspepsia of Melville's problematical whale, therefore, is something to be imagined with humorous relish and wide-eyed incredulity—once we understand, no, once we *feel*, the full humanity of the adjective. This humor, also captured by Hawthorne in his descriptions of the trampling of crow's feet and the prodigious gratulation of Chanticleer, is a strong potential in *prodigious*, since Humor and Surprise are sibling deities who sit high in the Olympus of the spirit.

If *prodigious* was less frequently used in the twentieth century than in the previous four, and it may have been, it was nonetheless still used, and used well. The word captures our sense of the startled and gives us a funny, toney juxtaposition that ordinary words such as *surprising* or *unusual* lack: a prodigious stench suffocates us, and a prodigious bulk leaves us gaping. It is easy to see why *prodigious* is a venerable and vigorous classic word that will be encountered by readers of all ages in most of the best books of the world.

7 acute

The English adjective *acute* comes from the Latin *acuere*, to sharpen. Today, fifteen centuries after the last vestiges of the western Roman Empire were vandalized for good, we still use our child of *acuere* to describe forms of sharpness. A sharp instrument can be acute, but so can a sharp mind. Sharp hearing is acute, and acute pains are sharp. A critical social crisis, such as a famine or a shortage of medical supplies, is acute. And as we all remember from our callow forays into geometry, an angle less than ninety degrees, like this <, is acute because its point is sharp, if you get the point.

Especially in the last three centuries, British and American authors have used acute to sharpen the sharpnesses in their novels and plays. In Jonathan Swift's acute 1726 satire on human foibles, *Gulliver's Travels*, he described acute judgment and animals whose behavior "was so orderly and rational, so acute and judicious." Gulliver observed, dryly, that the "more acute wits of Europe" had reduced politics into a science, and he found large creatures "whose large optics were not so acute as mine in viewing smaller objects."

In *Vindication of the Rights of Woman*, Mary Wollstonecraft described an acute observer. Observers, it seems, are frequently acute, for Jane Austen also observed them in *Pride and Prejudice*; Austen found a "most acute observer" and described "Elizabeth, who had expected to find in her as acute and unembarrassed an observer as ever Mr. Darcy had been." Austen wrote that "her head ached acutely," and she devised a tumultuous plot for her characters, "involving them both in misery of the acutest kind."

In 1826 James Fenimore Cooper found copious use for *acute* in his epic of forest and Indian warfare *The Last of the Mohicans*. Cooper described characters' "proverbial acuteness," "senses rendered doubly acute by the danger," "the experience and native acuteness of his commander," "acute and practiced intellects," and "a pang even more acute than any that her fears had excited." Cooper wrote that "His vision became more acute as the shades of evening settled on the place," and he extolled "Those acute and long practiced senses, whose powers so often exceed the limits of all ordinary credulity." He observed the sage Hawk-eye "examining the signs of the place with that acuteness which distinguished him." Moving silently through the forest, he "came to a halt, and listened for hostile sounds with an acuteness of organs that would be scarcely conceivable to a man in a less natural state."

In *The Scarlet Letter*, Nathaniel Hawthorne described a "crisis of acutest pain." He contrasted "exquisite pain, or pleasure as acute" and described "Pearl, with her remarkable precocity and acuteness." Hawthorne also used *acute* frequently in *The House of the Seven Gables*. He wrote about acute agony, acute endowments, and acute senses. In fact, Hawthorne's gables themselves are acute; Hawthorne depicted "a rusty wooden house, with seven acutely peaked gables." Humorously, he described "Hepzibah, who had been screwing her visual organs into the acutest focus of which they were capable"; later, she "screwed her dim optics to their acutest point, in the hopes of making out, with greater distinctness, a certain window."

In 1851, the same year that Hawthorne's *The House of the Seven Gables* was published, Harriet Beecher Stowe's *Uncle Tom's Cabin* set the reading public aflame with indignation over the suffering and misery of slavery. In her deliberately incendiary book, Stowe described a "dry, cautious acuteness," a "usual acuteness and good sense," and "an expression of great acuteness and shrewdness in his face." "There was," Stowe wrote, "a morbid sensitiveness and acuteness of feeling in me on all possible subjects." A decade after Stowe's intense antislavery novel, the flames would leap from her pages onto the battlefield, and John Brown's truth would go marchin' on.

An interesting example of *acute* comes from Charles Dickens, who, in his 1859 classic *A Tale of Two Cities*, described "a prolonged shock, of great acuteness." What, we wonder, are the properties of shock that would comprise acuteness?

George Eliot used *acute* in *Silas Marner*. The Squire replied with "a sudden acuteness which startled Godfrey," poor thing. And we learn, colloquially, that "it 'ud take a 'cute man to make a tale like that." We are alerted to "that criticism with which minds of extraordinary acuteness must necessarily contemplate the doings of their fallible fellow men." And we learn that even "Nancy, with all the acute sensibility of her own affections, shared her husband's view, that Marner was not justifiable in his wish."

George Eliot wrote *Silas Marner* in 1861. Fifteen years later, Henry James wrote *The American* and described "observation, acutely exercised," "acute preoccupation," "an ecstasy which the acutest misfortune might have been defied to dissipate," and more striking, "a glance of acute interrogation." In James's novel our hero, Newman, is enamored of Europeans' culture and refinement: "He had been struck with their acuteness, their subtlety, their tact, their felicity of judgment." Newman himself does not possess such felicities, and "his perception of the difference between good architecture and bad was not acute."

As the nineteenth century came to a close, numerous authors used *acute* to describe forms of sharpness. In *The Return of the Native*, Thomas Hardy described "ophthalmia in its acute form" and "an acuteness as extreme as it could be without verging on craft." In *Dr. Jekyll and Mr. Hyde*, Robert Louis Stevenson described "the acuteness of this remorse" and the "acuteness of the symptoms." Stephen Crane's young Henry Fleming, in *The Red Badge of Courage*, "developed the acute exasperation of a pestered animal" and looked about at his fellow soldiers to find that there "was an acute interest in all their faces." From all of us who have felt the acute exasperation of a pestered animal but didn't know how to put it into words, thank you, Stephen Crane. In 1898 H.G. Wells used *acute* wonderfully in his prescient classic *The War of the Worlds*: "The contrast between the swift and complex movements of these contrivances and the inert, panting clumsiness of their masters was acute." Well, the Martians have not landed, but for us poor earthlings, the contrast between our swift contrivances and our own panting clumsiness is still acute.

In the twentieth century, writers continued to use *acute* to indicate the sharp things of the world. In Kipling's 1901 novel *Kim*, we learn that "the Bengali suffered acutely in the flesh" and that "he was acutely aware of their cunning and their greed."

Joseph Conrad, in his 1902 masterpiece *Heart of Darkness*, used *acute* to form a haunting image of death, human misery, and starvation: "Near the same tree two more bundles of acute angles sat with their legs drawn up." Conrad also described "the crowd, of whose presence behind the curtain of trees I had been acutely conscious all the time."

Jack London used *acute* to describe the preternatural abilities of his dog-become-wolf Buck, whose "hearing developed such acuteness that in his sleep he heard the faintest sound."

In *The Great Gatsby*, F. Scott Fitzgerald described "those men who reach such an acute limited excellence at twenty-one that everything afterward savors of anticlimax." Fitzgerald's anticlimax could lead to a jaded form of emptiness for a character, "as if complacency, more acute than of old, was not enough to him any more."

George Orwell used *acute* in *Animal Farm*: "Every mouthful of food was an acute positive pleasure," and in *1984* to describe Winston Smith's enamorata, Julia: "In some ways she was far more acute than Winston, and far less susceptible to Party propaganda." In fact, she was, wrote Orwell, "capable of great acuteness."

In *Native Son*, Richard Wright described his character Bigger Thomas as "feeling acutely sorry."

For good reason, Neville Shute's doomed characters feel "acutely nervous" in *On the Beach*.

In her 1972 novel *Julie of the Wolves*, Jean Craighead George wrote that "Kapu wrinkled his brow and turned an ear to tune in more acutely on her voice." Wolves, it would seem, are chronic head-turners, for again, "He turned his head almost upside down to get a more acute focus on her."

In *Song of Solomon*, Toni Morrison wrote that "the longing to leave becomes acute."

And Eudora Welty, in the beautiful *One Writer's Beginnings*, used *acute* as a way of differentiating between prepositions: "Listening for them is something more acute than listening to them." "What the story 'June Recital' most acutely shows the reader," Welty wrote, "lies in her inner life."

And so the use of *acute* ranges from the literal—Hawthorne's acute gables—to the metaphorical—Wells's acute contrast—to the horrible—Conrad's brutally geometric bundles of acute angles.

There is, we become acutely aware, a potential universe of meaning within each word. This universe exists availably, waiting to be unlocked by the first mind to perceive its relationship to our particular situations. We have only to look, and we will see, everywhere about us, acute angles, acute minds, acute suffering, and acute senses. And in asking why we compare such things as intelligence and sensitivity to sharp angles, we are led to profound levels of self-understanding—to the realm of Socratic asking, where even a single word can reveal to us the nature of our own thinking.

8 clamor

The English noun *clamor* comes from the Latin *clamor* and the Latin verb *clamare*, to cry out. A clamor is no mild call; it is a loud outcry, a vociferous uproar, and especially one that continues vehemently. People *keep* clamoring. *Clamor* is a strong word; it cannot be wasted on any old fuss.

Four hundred years ago, when your great, great, great, great whoevers were doing whatever wherever, William Shakespeare used *clamor* in his plays to give strength and drama to his phrases. In 1594 he used *clamor* in *The Taming of the Shrew* to help Petruchio pester Katherine: "And with the clamor keep her still awake." In *Hamlet* we find an "instant burst of clamor," and in *Macbeth* we learn that the "obscure bird / Clamour'd the livelong night." The famous regicides plan to "make our griefs and clamour roar / Upon his death," and even the trumpets get into the act: "Make our trumpets speak; give them all breath, / Those clamorous harbingers of blood and death." And in *King Lear*, we meet the indignant and irate Kent, who threatens and excoriates the perfidious villain Oswald, "one whom I will beat into clamorous whining if thou deny'st the least syllable of thy addition." We long—how we long—for Oswald to deny a syllable of his addition, just one, for we would love to see Kent beat him into clamorous whining. Alas, it is Kent who is thrown into the stocks, and there is no justice in theater, especially when Shakespeare is pulling the strings of words.

In Milton's 1667 epic *Paradise Lost*, he described a scene "with terrors and with clamours compast round." The battle for Heaven commenced: "now storming fury rose, / And clamor such as heard in Heav'n till now / Was never." In fact, "the savage clamour drown' d / Both Harp and Voice." The clamors described in *Paradise Lost* on the bloody plains of Heaven and in the burning fires of Hell are so extreme that Milton coined a new word to describe them: *pandemonium*, the monstrous sound of all (*pan*) of the demons.

In Jane Austen's *Pride and Prejudice*, she described "the clamorous happiness of Lydia herself in bidding farewell." That was in 1813. In his 1820 novel *Ivanhoe*, Sir Walter Scott wrote about clamorous grief and clamorous applause. At one point, "all ranks joined in a clamorous shout of exultation," and even better, we are presented with "the clamorous yells and barking of all the dogs in the hall." Dogs, you see, are connoisseurs of clamor, and they know it more deeply than we do. Ask any dog, and he will tell you.

Scott was born in 1771 and was a friend of Wordsworth. *Ivanhoe* was a novel of Scott's maturity, written when he was fifty years old. Scott would live on until 1851. Like Wordsworth, he was a rapt observer of the 1789 French Revolution, a sanguinary episode in European history that coincided with the birth, across the Atlantic, of James Fenimore Cooper, who would write thrilling tales of pathfinders in leather stockings, hawk-eyed riflemen, and dangerous Indian tribes.

In *The Last of the Mohicans*, Cooper used *clamor* frequently to signify intense and prolonged outcries. "The clamorous noises again rushed down the island," he wrote. He described a "clamorous and weeping assemblage" and a character who "was interrupted by the clamor of a drum from the approaching Frenchmen." People are "mingling their different opinions and advice in noisy clamor," and the "clamor of many voices soon announced that a party approached."

The Brontës used *clamor* to loud effect. In *Jane Eyre*, Charlotte Brontë permitted "confusion to rise to clamor"—something that confusion is wont to do. Her sister Emily used *clamor* in *Wuthering Heights* to enhance the drama of dialogue: "'Hold your noise!' cried I hastily, enraged at her clamorous manner." Brontë also has a character "vociferate, more clamorously than before."

In 1850 Nathaniel Hawthorne eerily described "the clamor of fiends and night-hags" in *The Scarlet Letter*, and in the next year, 1851, he used *clamor* repeatedly in *The House of the Seven Gables*. Hawthorne wrote of the "clamor of the wind through the lonely house," of a "hateful clamor," and of a moment "when again the shop bell tinkled clamorously."

Also in 1851, Harriet Beecher Stowe wrote of characters "occasionally breaking out into clamorous explosions of delight" and of how the "clamor and confusion of the battle drew Miss Ophelia and St. Clare both to the spot."

In *Moby Dick*, also an 1851 work, Herman Melville's characters are "not clamorous for pardon."

It would be twenty-five years between these great works of 1851 and the emergence of Mark Twain in his 1876 classic *Tom Sawyer*. During this time, the clamorous, red god of war would sate his appetite on the fields of Gettysburg and Shiloh, a president would be assassinated, and the United States would suffer wounds and healing that would powerfully affect its future literature. Eventually, Mark Twain wrote of the "glad clamor of laughter," something that people needed to read. Twain described a character who "clamored up the homestretch," and he observed an expression of surprise that "was largely counterfeit and not as clamorous and effusive as it might have been under happier circumstances."

In 1895, thirty years after the dust had settled, young Stephen Crane, who was only twenty-four years old, used his imagination to artistically recreate the experience of the Civil War. In *The Red Badge of Courage*, Crane's callow protagonist, Henry Fleming, finds himself caught up in "a profound clamor" much louder and more terrifying than he had expected, surrounded by "clamors which came from many directions." Fleming is overwhelmed: "For a moment in the great clamor, he was like the proverbial chicken." He flees from the battle; eventually, his "ailments, clamoring, forced him to seek the place of food and rest."

In *The War of the Worlds*, H.G. Wells described "the clamor of bells."

In *Lord Jim*, Conrad depicted "human beings clamorous with the distress of cries for help"—help, we recall, that was not forthcoming. Later, in *Heart of Darkness*, Conrad wrote that "A complaining clamour, modulated in savage discords, filled our ears."

In *Kim*, Kipling wrote, beautifully, that "The clamor of Benares, oldest of all earth's cities awake before the Gods, day and night, beat round the walls as the sea's roar round a breakwater." Kipling heard "the clamor of the crows" and described how the "sleepers sprung to life, and the station filled with clamor and shoutings, cries of water and sweetmeat vendors."

Jack London, who in his turn-of-the-century photographs reminds us of Jack Kerouac, wrote of the call of the wild and of the dog Buck, who "did not steal for joy of it but because of the clamour of his stomach." There are times when the voice of the wild is loud, and a being is "deaf to all save the clamour for battle."

In his 1916 *A Portrait of the Artist as a Young Man,* the thick-spectacled James Joyce described his autobiographical alter ego, Stephen Daedalus, as a hypersensitive young artist, almost strangling in his own introspective giftedness, "his heart clamoring against his bosom in a tumult." Joyce described a "humble follower in the wake of clamorous conversions" and observed that the "inhuman clamor soothed his ears."

Reading experience teaches us to recognize the linguistic signature of an author, such as the unique originality and precision of F. Scott Fitzgerald's Jazz Age sentences. In *The Great Gatsby*, Fitzgerald described "groaning words that echoed clamorously through the bare garage" and then "the foreign clamor on the sidewalk." Fitzgerald did not know it, but the world was about to hear the clamor of the stock market as it crashed and crashed.

When the crash dust had cleared, Nobel Prize-winner Pearl Buck wrote her 1931 classic *The Good Earth*. Buck described the people and earth of China, with people "forever clamoring for sweet food" and a character "forever clamoring to sell that strip near to the western field we now have." "When the river burst again," Buck wrote, "the people went howling and clamoring to this magistrate's house."

In *Native Son*, Richard Wright wrote that the "clamor ceased," and he observed that his protagonist, Bigger Thomas, was imprisoned behind the bars of his own limitations: "His feelings clamored for an answer his mind could not give."

In George Orwell's 1945 *Animal Farm*, the animals "clamoured to be allowed to go out." In Orwell's *1984*, written in 1949, he described the sociology of want, in which "dozens of others clamored round the stall, accusing the stall keeper of favoritism" and in which Winston was driven to unintended actions because the "clamorous hunger in his belly seemed to justify him."

In *Invisible Man*, Ralph Ellison created a scene of isolation and disorientation, with characters "listening to the voice almost lost in the clamour of shouts, screams, burglar alarms, and silence." Depend upon Ellison to detect the clamor of silence.

From Henry Miller's 1953 *The Crucible*, we learn that "my heart has clamored intimations."

From William Golding's Rock-n-Roll Age *Lord of the Flies*, we learn that "Ralph's face was dark with breathlessness and the air over the island was full of bird-clamor and echoes ringing." "Jack started to protest," Golding wrote, "but the clamor changed from the general wish for a chief to an election by acclaim." After this, the boys follow their leader clamorously. Golding described the island, where "Tall trunks bore unexpected pale flowers all the way up to the dark canopy where life went on clamorously."

In *Catch-22*, Joseph Heller used *clamor* in his typically unpredictable way: "His head was throbbing from a shrill clamor that drilled relentlessly into both ears."

In *A Separate Peace*, John Knowles bid his characters prepare, "in case suitors begin clamoring at the door."

And in her softly brilliant 1983 retro-introspection *One Writer's Beginnings*, Eudora Welty described the clamor of curiosity: "From the first I was clamorous to learn—I wanted to know and begged to be told not so much what, or how, or why, or where as when."

Would the Romans—Ovid, for instance—be pleased with what we have done with their word? Probably. Twenty centuries have not dulled the intensity of this very human word. Somehow, it endured through a dark and stormy night of European Medievalism. It weathered the hordes of Visigoths and Gauls. It survived the Normans. In four centuries of our literature, in an Angle-ish language that did not exist when Ovid penned *The Metamorphoses*, we find clamorous happiness, grief, shouts, yells, whining, curiosity, harbingers, wind, explosions, noises, voices, laughter, ailments, bells, complaints, crows, dogs, stomachs, hearts, words, and feelings. There is even, courtesy of Ralph Ellison, a clamorous silence. Life, we infer, is filled with clamor.

The vigor, creative adaptability, and humanity of this word would seem to promise that in two more millennia, when English is an arcane ancient language, replaced by a future tongue yet unnamed, our linguistic descendants will still listen to a long, complaining uproar and call it a clamor.

9 exquisite

Like many modern English words, the adjective *exquisite* is a surviving artifact from the ancient Roman Empire. Coming from the Latin *exquirere*, to search out, *exquisite* is a descendant of the stems *ex*, out, and *quaerere*, to ask. In other words, *exquisite* is a relative of the dread noun *inquisition*. Today, we use *exquisite* to indicate many different things that may at first seem unrelated; something that is exquisite may be exceptionally beautiful or lovely, or it may be intricate and elaborate, or it may be of superb quality. When applied to people, *exquisite* may indicate great sensitivity or fastidiousness. It may even indicate intensity, as in an exquisite pain.

What would an exquisite pain have to do with an exquisite design or exquisite taste in art? We must return to the original idea behind *exquisite*: what is exquisite is *unusual*—so unusual that it must be *searched out*. When we encounter what is truly difficult to find, what is truly rare, then we have found the exquisite. In literature we find exquisite gowns, exquisite sensations, and exquisite echoes. There are exquisite attitudes and exquisite agonies, exquisite sensibilities and exquisite images. From Shakespeare's *Romeo and Juliet* to Joseph Heller's *Catch-22*, American and British authors have used *exquisite* to indicate the exceptional, whether positive or negative.

In 1792 Mary Wollstonecraft used *exquisite* in her *Vindication of the Rights of Woman* to describe the "impressions made by exquisite senses," an "exquisite sensibility," and a "most exquisitely polished instinct." Wollstonecraft remarked with some irony, "I have seen also an eye glanced coldly over a most exquisite picture rest, sparkling with pleasure, on a caricature rudely sketched."

In *Pride and Prejudice*, written in 1813, Jane Austen used *exquisite* to indicate musical talent: "Her performance on the piano-forte is exquisite."

Mary Shelley used *exquisite* in her 1816 novel *Frankenstein* to describe "the exquisite beauty of the Arabian," the "exquisite pleasure in dwelling on the recollections of childhood," and "meadows of exquisite verdure." Victor Frankenstein complained of his monster that "he destroyed my friends; he devoted to destruction beings who possessed exquisite sensations, happiness, and wisdom." The monster sought "as exquisite and divine a retreat as Pandaemonium appeared to the demons of hell after their sufferings in the lake of fire."

In 1826, ten years later and an ocean to the west, James Fenimore Cooper used *exquisite* in his leatherstocking tale *The Last of the Mohicans*. Cooper's characters possess "the singular compound of quick, vigilant sagacity and exquisite simplicity" and communicate through the forest with unusual sounds: "The notes were in the extremes of human sounds; being sometimes melancholy and exquisitely plaintive, even rivalling the melody of birds." Taking a turn to the grotesque, Cooper described how a victor "passed the knife around the exquisitely molded head of his victim." Cooper observed characters molded with "exquisite proportions" and a "countenance that was exquisitely regular and dignified," and he noted one who "might easily have been converted by the imagination into an exquisite and faultless representation of the warlike deity of his tribe."

Nathaniel Hawthorne, writing twenty-five years after Cooper's Hawk-eye chronicles, described "exquisite pain" and "exquisite suffering" in the 1850 classic *The Scarlet Letter*. In *The House of the Seven Gables*, written one year later, Hawthorne described "exquisite taste," and he captured the essence of *exquisite* in a way rarely equaled: "His feeling for flowers was very exquisite, and seemed not so much a taste as an emotion." Hawthorne also used *exquisite* to describe the sound of the voice: "Her tone, as she uttered the exclamation, had a plaintive and really exquisite melody thrilling through it."

The same year, Harriet Beecher Stowe used *exquisite* in her urgent *Uncle Tom's Cabin*. Stowe found "Two or three exquisite paintings of children" and described characters "snapping their fingers and flourishing their heels with exquisite delight." She also used the word as a noun, describing a "young exquisite" who was "slapping the shoulder of a sprucely dressed young man."

Twenty-five years later in 1876, another American, Henry James, used *exquisite* abundantly in *The American*, his account of a practical New World soul adventuring in the cosmopolitan perils of European society. James observed "an exquisite touch in a pianist," "an exquisite work" of art, "so exquisite a compound," "an exquisite sense of beauty," and people who were "exquisitely organized." James's American had "no very exquisite sense of comfort or convenience" and felt himself a member of "that small and superior class—that exquisite group—composed of persons who are worthy to remain unmarried." James observed how "his travelling back to Milan only to get into a deeper muddle appeared...exquisitely and ludicrously just." Strikingly, James described a character who "was an exquisite image of shabby gentility" and noted with some doubt that Mrs. Tristram "then undertook to be exquisitely agreeable."

In his 1878 *The Return of the Native*, Thomas Hardy wondered "by what right a being of such exquisite finish had been placed in circumstances calculated to make of her charms a curse rather than a blessing."

In *Dr. Jekyll and Mr. Hyde*, Robert Louis Stevenson used *exquisite* to enhance the feeling of fear: "my blood was changed into something exquisitely thin and icy."

Few have ever used words as well as Oscar Wilde, and in *The Picture of Dorian Gray*, Wilde, who once said that the British and the Americans have everything in common except language, used *exquisite* exquisitely. Wilde observed that "Behind every exquisite thing that existed, there was something tragic." He described "chiseled lips curled in exquisite disdain" and noted that Lord Henry "found an exquisite pleasure in playing on the lad's unconscious egotism." Wilde ironically described "exquisite temptations that we had not the courage to yield to," noted that "There was an exquisite poison in the air," and wrote, accurately describing himself through his character, that "I had a strange feeling that Fate had in store for me exquisite joys and exquisite sorrows."

In *The Red Badge of Courage*, written thirty years after the Civil War ended, young Stephen Crane brilliantly described young Henry Fleming, who ran from imagined Death and returned to face mere death and whose exertions took their toll: "An exquisite drowsiness had spread through him."

In his 1895 *The Time Machine*, H.G. Wells told the story of the Time Traveller, inventor of a device so incredible that even his best friends were incredulous. The Time Traveller propelled himself into the distant future, where the species *Homo sapiens sapiens* had divided into two descendent species, the dreaded Morlocks and the beautiful but weak

Eloi. At one point the Time Traveller finds "eight or ten of these exquisite creatures."

Joseph Conrad used his second language, English, so exquisitely that his works became classics. In *Lord Jim*, written in 1900, Conrad repeatedly referred to exquisite sensibilities. "This," he wrote, "was their criticism on his exquisite sensibility." He acutely described "an exquisite sensibility that makes certain silences more lucid than speeches." Beautifully, Conrad described a butterfly that "spread out dark bronze wings...with exquisite white veinings." And in his 1902 *Heart of Darkness*, he found poetry in the horizon: "The day was ending in a serenity of still and exquisite brilliance."

In 1903 Jack London used *exquisite* in his tale of Northern wilderness, cruelty, and freedom, *The Call of the Wild*. For Buck, the dog whose tame personality is gradually transformed into a feral intensity, "Every part, brain and body, nerve tissue and fibre, was keyed to the most exquisite pitch." Buck passes through many trials, but "All the pain he had endured was as nothing compared with the exquisite agony of this."

In James M. Barrie's *Peter Pan*, we meet immortal characters. One could fit in the palm of the hand: "It was a girl called Tinker Bell exquisitely gowned in a skeleton leaf." Barrie wrote that "No woman, however large, could have had a more exquisite boudoir and bedchamber combined." More soberly, Barrie described the "exquisite tortures to which they were to put him at break of day."

In her 1911 novel *Ethan Frome*, Edith Wharton described the genesis of a romance: "And there were other sensations, less definable but more exquisite, which drew them together with a shock of silent joy."

James Joyce, in *A Portrait of the Artist as a Young Man*, asked, "Isn't she an exquisite creature?"

One British writer who used *exquisite* extensively was E.M. Forster. In the ambiguous and disturbing *A Passage to India*, Forster wrote, "There are some exquisite echoes in India." He described Dr. Aziz as "exquisitely dressed, from tie-pin to spats." "In Europe," he observed, "life retreats out of the cold, and exquisite fireside myths have resulted— Balder, Persephone—but here the retreat is from the source of life." Forster described "exquisite nebulae, shadings fainter than the tail of a comet or the midday moon." Three ladies, Forster wrote, "suddenly shot out of the summer-house like exquisitely colored swallows, and salaamed them." And with respect, Forster defined "Islam, an attitude towards life both exquisite and durable."

In *The Bridge of San Luis Rey*, written in 1927, Thornton Wilder used *exquisite* to describe "an exquisite daughter" and exquisite ideas in language: "But what divine Spanish he speaks and what exquisite things he says in it!" Wilder described "the exquisite sensibility of the Letters" and observed, "It is true that the Limeans were given to interpolating trivial songs into the most exquisite comedies."

In 1949, George Orwell wrote about 1984, and in *1984* he described "cream-papered walls and white wainscoting, all exquisitely clean."

And in 1955 Joseph Heller used *exquisite* in *Catch-22* to describe the thrill we feel when we hear words used well: "The skilled choice of words he was exercising was exquisitely titillating."

Like Forster's *India*, the adjective *exquisite* itself contains some exquisite echoes that resound to us from the far corners of English and American literature. In our experience, we encounter many things that are exceptionally unusual, for better or for worse, and we live in the tension between the exquisitely good and the exquisitely bad.

10 languor

The English noun *languor* is yet another example of the ancient world speaking through modern lips; we think of *languor* as our word, but of course it is theirs—the Romans, I mean. When we use *languor*, or *languid*, or *languish*, or even *languorous*, we are sustaining an old, old echo of the Latin verb *languere*, to languish. For us, as for Virgil and his friends, *languor* is a lack of energy. It is torpor. It is lassitude. The lethargy of languor can be physical, as in the languor of napping lions on the Serengetti, or it can be mental, as in the languor of trying to be attentive to a tedious, soporific, and meaningless desultory tirade. To languish is to descend into languor, to waste away.

Judging from the presence of *languor* in literature, there is a heavy presence of languor in life. The poet John Berryman—bless his suffering soul—once intoned, "Life, friends, is boring, though we must not say so." And Hamlet, in his existential languor, observed how weary, stale, flat, and unprofitable are all the uses of this world. Just thinking of *that* makes us languish, does it not? Well, I can't speak for you.

What writers would you guess have resorted to *languor* most frequently? Would you expect it less often from modern writers than from Victorian novelists? Would you feel affirmed to find it in *Frankenstein* but surprised to find it in Hemingway's simple, declarative monosyllabism? Would it plunge you into cognitive dissonance to find *languor* in something jazzy and jaded, like Joseph Heller's *Catch-22*?

Maybe not. But we do find *languor* in British and American literature for four hundred years. In fact, if we look back to 1596 and see what was up in the gloaming of the sixteenth century, we find Will Shakespeare toiling away on *Romeo and Juliet* in twinkling London, writing that "One desp'rate grief cures with another's languish."

In the four centuries since, *languor-languid-languish-languorous* has been used by Milton, Shelley, the Brontës, Hawthorne, Stowe, Melville, Dickens, James, Twain, Hardy, Stevenson, Wilde (the most predictable of all), Conrad, Grahame, Wharton, Burnett, Joyce, Forster, Fitzgerald, Hemingway, Buck, Ellison, Heller, Knowles, and Morrison.

And others.

These writers described languid everything: languid expressions, languid gestures, and languid replies. F. Scott Fitzgerald, for example, used *languid* to signify the jaded opulence of the Jazz Age: "Slenderly, languidly, their hands set lightly on their hips, the two young women preceded us." But languor is not always to be envied: "His wife," Fitzgerald wrote—and he must have sat back in satisfaction at his sentence—"was shrill, languid, handsome, and horrible." What a complex of characteristics.

Every writer loves certain words and will return to them over and again. Mary Wollstonecraft, writing her *Vindication of the Rights of Woman* in 1792, relied on *languor* repeatedly. She described a life "lost in feverish pleasures or wearisome languor" and wondered how anyone could "supinely dream life away in the lap of pleasure, or the languor of weariness." She described "languid, yet tranquil spirits" and objected that women must "ever languish like exotics, and be reckoned beautiful flaws in nature." And she explained that for a woman whose life is not respected, "her desire of pleasing will then grow languid."

Wollstonecraft's daughter, Mary Shelley, used *languor* in *Frankenstein*. The monster sinks "to the ground through languor and extreme weakness." He feels "languid, and unable to reflect on all that has passed." He describes "the expressive eyes of Henry, languishing in death, the dark orbs covered by the lids, the long black lashes that fringed them." And Victor Frankenstein discovers the monster's terrible work: "the deadly languor and coldness of the limbs told me, that what I now held in my arms had ceased to be the Elizabeth whom I had loved."

Another writer who loved *languor* was Joseph Conrad. In Conrad's raw-nerved novels, *languor* becomes sensitized and filled with what Eliot would have called insidious intent. In *Heart of Darkness*, Conrad described "the oily and languid sea," "the languid beat of the stern-wheel" that "flopped languidly," "his collected languid manner," and "the composed languor of his expression." A composed languor—here is a novel's worth of meaning bounded in the nutshell of a single phrase. In *Heart of Darkness*, "White men with long staves in their hands appeared languidly from amongst the buildings." In *Lord Jim*, Conrad described "the fingers of a languid hand," "a pleasurable languor running through every limb," and the suffocating stillness in which "there was hardly more than a languid stir of air in the place." Conrad noted that things could be "too pleasurably languid," and he plumbed levels of suggestion, describing how "After this we remained silent and languid for a time as if exhausted." In a single phrase, Conrad summed up the pervasive weariness and defeat of *Lord Jim*: his characters live and die amid "the languor of the earth."

Wollstonecraft, Shelley, and Conrad are not the only writers who have used *languor*. In 1667—we forget that

Milton wrote *Paradise Lost* more than three hundred years ago—Milton described "languisht hope reviv'd." In *Jane Eyre*, Charlotte Brontë described "the languid elegance of Lord Ingram," and her sister Emily described "large languid eyes" in *Wuthering Heights*. "Linton's looks and movements," Emily Brontë added, "were very languid." She wrote that "his large blue eyes wandered timidly over her, the hollowness round them transforming to haggard wildness the languid expression they once possessed."

In *The Scarlet Letter*, Nathaniel Hawthorne languidly described an "interest in this worn-out subject languidly reviving itself," and he observed "an inevitable and weary languor." His friend Melville, in his leviathan tome, wrote that "everything resolves you into languor." In Mark Twain's *Tom Sawyer*, "Most of the pupils glanced up languidly," a phenomenon remembered by every teacher who has braved out a dull day. And Henry James, in *The American*, ironically described a character who, "with her eight years in Paris, talked of herself as a languid Oriental." Can one be a languid Occidental, one wonders, or are all Occidentals sprightly?

Harriet Beecher Stowe liked *languor*. In *Uncle Tom's Cabin*, "She opened her eyes in a state of dreamy, delicious languor," and "he lay languidly opening and shutting his eyes." Stowe wrote of languid politeness, languid kisses, and a character who was "leaning her head languidly on her hand."

With his characteristic beauty and economy of word, Robert Louis Stevenson used *languor* in *Treasure Island* to describe how "the boom of the distant surges disturbed the languor of the afternoon," and in *Dr. Jekyll and Mr. Hyde*, he described one "languidly weak both in body and mind."

By the booming surges of the Atlantic, Stevenson's contemporary Thomas Hardy used *languor* to suggest the bleak world—weariness of the *fin de siècle*. In Hardy's *The Return of the Native*, Eustacia Vye murmurs languidly, droops to languor again, and answers "with languid calmness, artificially maintained." Hardy observed that "her apparent languor did not arise from lack of force"; "One point was evident in this; that she had been existing in a suppressed state, and not in one of languor, or stagnation." Eustacia is a deep character; we look into her as into a pool: "Clym then went into the garden; and a thoughtful languor stole over Eustacia for the remainder of the afternoon." It is no wonder that Eustacia Vye was Holden Caulfield's favorite literary character; she moves through the pages with such reality that the novel is like Marianne Moore's definition of poems: imaginary gardens with real toads in them. *The Return of the Native* is an imaginary novel with a real Eustacia in it.

Thomas Hardy also used *languor* in *The Mayor of Casterbridge*, where characters answer languidly and where "the game usually languished for the aforesaid reason."

Oscar Wilde, who used any word he liked, used *languor* in his jaded classic of overexperience *The Picture of Dorian Gray*. Wilde wrote of "dreamy languorous eyes" and languid speech, but only in an Oscar Wilde novel could we find a sentence such as: "the heavy lilac blooms, with their clustering stars, moved to and fro in the languid air."

In his brilliantly vicarious *The Red Badge of Courage*, the precocious Stephen Crane described "the youth's languid fingers." The youth was, of course, Henry Fleming, whose mom told him not to try to fight the whole battle by himself. He should have listened; Moms know. In the bloody course of things, Henry was able to get some rest, and the "warm comfort of the blanket enveloped him and made a gentle languor."

H.G. Wells described a Martian invasion of the earth in *The War of the Worlds*. As the Martians methodically destroy England, the first person anonymous protagonist struggles to survive, but without promise: "My movements were languid, my plans of the vaguest."

In modern literature, *languor* has been used by Kenneth Grahame to describe Toad's languid replies, by Edith Wharton to describe how "Ethan, with a touch of his whip, roused the sorrel to a languid trot," and by James Joyce in *A Portrait of the Artist as a Young Man* to describe languid weariness, the languor of sleep, the languor and supple movement of music, and languid grace. Forster, in *A Passage to India*, described how "the singers' expressions became fatuous and languid."

In Wilder's *The Bridge of San Luis Rey*, a "tall, rather languorous beauty entered the room," and "she cultivated a delicate and languid magdelinism, as a great lady might." Of course, cultivating a languid magdelinism is something rarely attempted.

Pearl Buck is the last American woman before Toni Morrison to win the Nobel Prize in Literature. In her timeless novel of humanity's humanity, *The Good Earth*, her weary character "came suddenly out of her languor" and spoke weakly.

In Ralph Ellison's moody marginal-man classic *Invisible Man*, we read his poetic description of "the growing sound of a record shop loudspeaker blaring a languid blues." So much for the dichotomy between poetry and prose. As if that weren't enough, Ellison wrote, in the same book no less, that "It was a dream fall, my body languid and fastidious as to where to land, until the floor became impatient and smashed up to meet me." Anyone wondering why *Invisible Man* is a classic of American literature may read these two sentences and be edified.

Joseph Heller, in his sassy and sesquipedalian modern novel *Catch-22*, used *languor* lavishly. His character points "languidly toward the wall" and gestures "languidly toward his gigantic map of Italy." Heller described how "the officer without insignia cautioned with a languid restraining wave" and how he "began molesting his angular, pale, dissolute face languidly and coquettishly."

In *Song of Solomon*, Toni Morrison observed that it "was strange, the languorous, limp hand coming to rest at her side while her breathing was coming so quick and fast."

Tell the truth: Would you have expected *languor* to be one of the great classic words? And yet you see that it is. *Languor* is unexpectedly close to the bone, an essential contrary of its anti-particle energy. As human beings, we live in an ever-shifting languor-energy continuum, and we need this word to describe our lives. Writers from Shakespeare to Morrison have used *languor* to describe our myriad states of weakness, of phlegmatic lassitude, of exhaustion: physical, mental, moral, and cultural. Kenneth Clark, whom we honor in our memories, repeatedly turned, in his epochal *Civilisation* series, to the idea of energy, vitality, vigor. Being lively and alert like the Renaissance Florentines was, in Clark's mind, central to being civilized. Falling into sterile languor, lacking the will to build or think or fight or plan, was fatal to the spirit of civilization. Clark quoted the modern Greek poet Cavafy's great poem "Waiting for the Barbarians" to illustrate the status of the weary: in Cavafy's poem, languid Roman citizens are eager for the barbarian invasion—it would be better than nothing.

But soft, a languid weariness stills my hands, and my mind languishes into a lackadaisical lassitude. Tremulous, I sink into a phlegmatic torpor, and O, a leaden languor leans me back, and I must leave. Adieu, adieu, remember me.

11 grotesque

In his poem "Disillusionment of Ten O'Clock," the American poet Wallace Stevens longs for the creativity and imagination that are missing in our lives; he regrets that the houses are haunted by white night-gowns. None of them are strange, he complains, with socks of lace and beaded ceintures. Only here and there, Stevens thinks, an old sailor, drunk and asleep in his boots, catches tigers in red weather. Well, there *is* a place for the strange, and many strange things can be found beside the word *grotesque*.

The English adjective *grotesque* is one of the best stories in diction. We use *grotesque* to describe things that are ugly, unnatural, or fantastic, such as incongruous artistic combinations of animals, human beings, and vegetation. But *grotesque* literally means grotto-esque—grotto-like! A grotto is a cave, a cavern, or a subterranean chamber, and *grotto* comes from the Italian *grotta*, which comes from the Latin *crypta*, an underground passage. So what is the connection between weirdness and caves? Why would we describe weird art or ugly incongruity as grotto-like?

Blame it on Nero, the most despised tyrant in Western history. Although he apparently did not fiddle while Rome burned, he did squander Rome's wealth on his *domus aureus*, his great golden palace, which became an embarrassment to subsequent emperors, who knocked it down and built over the rubble. Centuries later, in the Renaissance, workmen discovered open passages under the ground that proved to be buried rooms of Nero's golden palace. Peering in, they saw, like Howard Carter peeping through a hole at Tutankhamen's tomb, wonderful things. Vague images in the shadows. Wall paintings of bizarre faces and forms. Weird shapes. They could almost hear the chuckles of dusty Roman ghosts. The discovery was so exciting that the painter Raphael had himself lowered down into the grotto so that he could see the ancient pagan art.

The fantastic wall paintings of Nero's grottos became known in Renaissance Italy as *grottesca*, the grotto-style, and ergo (argle, a Shakespearean buffoon would say), we have the modern English adjective *grotesque*, a gift to our language from art history.

If *grotesque* is an adjective that means weird, incongruous, or unnatural, then what nouns might this adjective modify? Well, in English and American literature, we find grotesque hats, grotesque masks, grotesque conceits, and a grotesque pallor. There is a grotesque performance, a grotesque dread of mirrors, and a grotesque grin. There are even grotesque songs.

Grotesque has been used by authors as modern as John Gardner and by authors as remote as John Milton. Joseph Heller used it, as did Ralph Ellison, Sylvia Plath, F. Scott Fitzgerald, Edith Wharton, Joseph Conrad, and H.G. Wells. The British writer Oscar Wilde used it, as did American writers such as Henry James, Herman Melville, and Harriet Beecher Stowe.

In 1667, which is now more than three centuries ago, John Milton used *grotesque* in *Paradise Lost* to describe a steep wilderness, with "hairy sides / With thicket overgrown, grotesque and wild." Milton must have realized that attributing overgrown hairy sides to a wilderness was itself a grotesque image.

James Fenimore Cooper, in *The Last of the Mohicans*, used *grotesque* to convey the fearsome shock of a war-painted face: "It was impossible to discover the expression of his features through the grotesque mask of paint under which they were concealed."

Charlotte Brontë described a "foreigner harsh and grotesque" in *Jane Eyre*, and her sister Emily reported "a quantity of grotesque carving" in *Wuthering Heights*.

In *The House of the Seven Gables*, Nathaniel Hawthorne brilliantly applied *grotesque* to an array of dissimilar things; he described "a china tea set painted over with grotesque figures of man, bird, and beast, in as grotesque a landscape." There is, he wrote, "a long, grotesque, and occasionally awestriking account of the carpenter's incantations" and a "will, most unlike her own, [that] constrained her to do its grotesque and fantastic bidding." Hawthorne described the fantastic appearance of the house: "Its whole visible exterior was ornamented with quaint figures, conceived in the grotesqueness of a Gothic fancy." One of the characteristics of literary genius is this—the profound love of a word that allows an author to see its resonances ricocheting from thing to thing. Hawthorne saw the grotesqueness of painted figures, of an awestriking story, of the fantastic bidding of a will, and of a Gothic fancy. And yes, Hawthorne also used *grotesque* in *The Scarlet Letter*. Read, and see what "grotesque horror" is there.

In *Uncle Tom's Cabin*, Harriet Beecher Stowe described "wild, grotesque songs" and explained how a character "could cut cunning little baskets out of cherry stones, could make grotesque faces on hickory-nuts." Again, the writer's power: we might expect *grotesque* to describe faces, but what stretch of mind, what synthesis and comparison, is involved in Stowe's perception of grotesque songs? If *grotesque* begins as an adjective to describe the weird and fantastic visions on a grotto wall, what is indicated by the sound of a grotesque song? How would a grotesque song sound different from a song that was not grotesque? Words may begin with limited and specialized meanings, but it is not long before creative and experimental minds begin stretching and extending them to new meanings that were scarcely imaginable by those who first constructed them.

In 1851, the same year that Harriet Beecher Stowe wrote *Uncle Tom's Cabin*, Herman Melville published *Moby Dick*, the *King Lear* of American literature. In *Moby Dick*, there is a carved lid "with all manner of grotesque figures and drawings," and there are "centaurs, griffins, and dolphins, similar to the grotesque figures on the celestial globe of the moderns." Whether dolphins would be upset at being included with grotesque centaurs and griffins is a question yet to be answered.

Henry James loved to use *grotesque*. In *The American*, he described "grotesque idols and fetiches [that] were sometimes taken out of their temples and carried abroad in golden chariots to be displayed to the multitude." "My pictures are grotesque," he wrote, and he described a character "as if he too were a large grotesque in a rather vulgar system of chamber-decoration." He noted that for one character, "to muffle herself in ascetic rags and entomb herself in a cell, was a confounding combination of the inexorable and the grotesque." James's American traveler abroad, Newman, had a certain sensitivity to wealth: "It mortified him, moreover, to think that Valentin lacked money; there was a painful grotesqueness in it." Newman "found in a curiosity-shop a grotesque little statuette in ivory" and asked whether another character was religious "in a tone which gave the inquiry a grotesque effect."

In Mark Twain's *Tom Sawyer*, there is "grotesque foolishness." Now, what does Twain mean? Where is he leading our thought? Foolishness, we think, is always foolish. For foolishness to become grotesque, it would have to become foolisher, even foolishest.

The English writer Thomas Hardy introduced us to the twentieth century with his sense of the strange. In the bleak twigs of the English landscape, he detected the nineteenth century's corpse outleant, and in *The Return of the Native*, he captured the chill wind of modernism: "Those whom Nature had depicted as merely quaint became the grotesque, the grotesque became preternatural; for all was in extremity." In *The Mayor of Casterbridge*, Hardy described how a "grotesque grin shaped itself on Henchard's face."

Oscar Wilde had a special fondness for the word *grotesque* and used it copiously in his grotesque novel *The Picture of Dorian Gray*. Wilde wrote that his characters were "as grotesque as the scenery" and that the "waving of crooked, false-jeweled fingers gave grotesqueness to the words." Wilde described "that somewhat grotesque dread of mirrors" and brilliantly told how "the imagination, made grotesque by terror, twisted and distorted as a living thing by pain, danced like some foul puppet on a stand." He observed "the vivid life that lurks in all grotesques, and that lends to Gothic art its enduring vitality." We read that "He had seen grotesque children huddled upon doorsteps, and heard shrieks and oaths from gloomy courts." "Three times," Wilde wrote, "the outstretched arms shot up convulsively, waving grotesque stiff-fingered hands in the air," and there was "the thing whose grotesque, misshapen shadow on the spotted carpet showed him that it had not stirred." Perhaps here, in Wilde's vivid sentences, is our closest approach to the center of the word *grotesque*; we find grotesque, stiff-fingered hands and grotesque, misshapen shadows. The carnival freak-show tone of *grotesque* emerges, and we see shadowy silhouettes and distorted outlines; unnatural sounds and threatening unknowns surround us. We are in the middle of the unknown, the landscape of the grotesque.

One of the most memorable uses of *grotesque* is by the young Stephen Crane, who never fought in the Civil War, being born in 1871, but who described the fighting so well that veterans relived their own experiences in his descriptions. Once the battle broke out, death came fast, and "Other men, punched by bullets, fell in grotesque agonies." Amidst the roar of battle, men found their "words coming unconsciously...in grotesque exclamations." We can only admire the superb poetry of Crane's "punched by bullets."

In H.G. Wells's novels, the reader is confronted by grotesque images of the future. In *The Time Machine*, "Great shapes like big machines rose out of the dimness, and cast grotesque black shadows." The Time Traveller describes himself as "dressed in dingy nineteenth-century garments, looking grotesque enough, garlanded with flowers." In *The War of the Worlds*, "huge black shapes, grotesque and strange, moved busily to and fro" as the Martians built their fighting machines in their crater. Wells described the panicked crowd with incisive perspicacity: "The man was running...and selling his papers for a shilling as he ran—a grotesque mingling of profit and panic." Wells described the grotesque changes of the day, the common contrasts of that grotesque time, and the "Grotesque gleam of a time no history will every fully describe!" He told how terrified characters trapped by the Martians in a house "would race across the kitchen in a grotesque way between eagerness and the dread of making a noise, and strike each other." The Martian invasion seems incredible, but Wells gathered us in: "Grotesque and foolish as this will seem to the sober reader, it is absolutely true."

In *Lord Jim*, Joseph Conrad described "grotesque and distinct visions" and "tragic or grotesque mysteries." "It was," he wrote, "an inexpressibly grotesque and vile performance." You might expect something more lurid in Conrad's *Heart of Darkness*, which sounded the anthem note of the disturbed modern era, and you do find something more lurid; you find a "bony head that nodded with grotesque jerks." Conrad also described how "they had faces like grotesque masks."

In *Ethan Frome*, Edith Wharton wrote about "the segregation of grotesquely muffled groups." And Forster, in *A Passage to India*—that puzzling book about a "grotesque incident"—found what was "Absolutely impossible, grotesque," as though he were describing Cyrano's nose.

The glamorous and gloomed F. Scott Fitzgerald used grotesque in *The Great Gatsby*. There was "a fantastic farm where ashes grow like wheat into ridges and hills and grotesque gardens." Too sensitive for his own good, Fitzgerald gave us one of our best visual images of grotesqueness: "I see it as a night scene by El Greco: a hundred houses, at once conventional and grotesque, crouching under a sullen, overhanging sky and a lustreless moon." The corruptwardly mobile Jay Gatsby is a tormented character who "found what a grotesque thing a rose is" and who was haunted at night by the "most grotesque and fantastic conceits" as he "tossed half-sick between grotesque reality and savage, frightening dreams."

In *The Bridge of San Luis Rey*, Thornton Wilder described a "grotesque old woman" and a character's "grotesque pallor." He described how the "almost grotesque and hungry face became beautiful."

Ralph Ellison, writing at the beginning of what Marlon Brando called the Brylcream Era, used *grotesque* to describe the Invisible Man's doings: "I shook him violently, seeing his head wobble grotesquely." "His triple-hatted head," Ellison wrote, showed "grotesquely atop the stoop."

In William Golding's feral *Lord of the Flies*, the abandoned boys gleefully "inched the grotesque dead thing up the rock and toppled it over on top."

Perhaps having an acute sense of the absurd leads one to perceive the grotesque in life. Joseph Heller's modern sense of the absurd is a salient characteristic in his *Catch-22*, where "Everything seemed strange, so tawdry and grotesque," where "They were grotesque, like useless young men in a depression," where "The silence was grotesque," and where "the chaplain wailed softly in a quavering voice, squinting with grotesque contortions of anguish and incomprehension." In *Catch-22*, "Yossarian gawked at Doc Daneeka in grotesque dismay" and "spied the chaplain standing close by gawking at him grotesquely in tortured wonder." Eventually, "He lost patience entirely with the whole grotesque and incomprehensible melee." Heller's world is grotesque; it is something at which we, and all its characters, gawk.

No sentimentalist herself, Sylvia Plath deliberately described, in *The Bell Jar*, "A woman not five feet tall, with a grotesque, protruding stomach." E.L. Doctorow, in *Ragtime*, wrote that "Days passed before he realized that the grotesque mimic on Murderer's Row had to have been the killer Harry K. Thaw." And Toni Morrison wrote in *Song of Solomon* that "Even a traveling show would have rejected her, since her freak quality lacked that important ingredient—the grotesque."

John Gardner, who told the monster's side of the story in *Grendel*, used *grotesque*. "Near Hrothgar's hall," Gardner's monster explains, "stand the images of the Scyldings' gods, grotesque faces carved out of wood or hacked from stone and set up in a circle." Grendel finds himself confronting his human enemy, "Staring at his grotesquely muscled shoulders—stooped, naked despite the cold." "I scream," he narrates, "grotesquely shaking hands."

Author upon author, century upon century, the uses of *grotesque* accumulate, and the examples we have seen are only a thin sample; the other authors and the other books also rely on this word to express what is bizarre and disturbing, odd and unnatural, weird and abnormal. We might have expected some authors, such as Heller and Wilde, to rely heavily on *grotesque*, and they did, but we might not have expected so many authors to use it so frequently.

Why does *grotesque* have such prominence in our language? Perhaps it is because the normal, being expected, requires little comment, whereas abnormal experiences merit explanation. Perhaps it is because we are drawn to the unusual as a relief from the tedium of our coffee-spoon lives. Perhaps wild things make our hearts sing. Whatever the reason, literature is filled with grotesque things: grins and scenery, times and exclamations, faces and accounts, foolishness and foreigners. And in this literature we see, once again, the ability of a right word to reflect for us the world that we inhabit.

12 condescend

If the universe is a vast Rube Goldberg machine, with concatenations of effects rippling from their causes and becoming the new causes of new effects, tripping and flipping the dominoes of phenomena in myriad and unpredictable ways, like perpetual motion pool balls, then perhaps even today the old echoes of Roman voices on the Appian Way from Rome to Brundisium are affecting effects.

And of course, when English-speaking peoples use words such as *condescend*, that is precisely what is happening. Ever since the gloaming of the Greek civilization, when some Roman wordsmith fixed the prefixes *con* (together) and *de* (down) to the beginning of the verb *scandere* (to climb) to form *condescendere*, Roman and post-Roman citizens such as ourselves have mouthed and remouthed the pattern: *con-de-scend*. In Spanish, it survives as *condescender*.

To condescend (the noun form is *condescension*) is to stoop to another's lower level, to climb (*scend*) down (*de*) with (*con*) him, to voluntarily waive superiority and assume equality with an inferior. As one would imagine, *condescend* is a verb that oscillates with complex potential; the inferior condescended to may not be amused by the lofty personage condescending, unless, of course, the inferior believes in his inferiority and regards himself as honored by the condescension. In Jane Austen's *Pride and Prejudice*, that is precisely the debased position of the odious lackey Mr. Collins, Elizabeth Bennet's obsequious cousin, who prostrates himself before the mere mention of his esteemed patroness, the supercilious Lady Catherine De Bourgh: "Such affability, such condescension," Collins gushes, as Austen's other characters repulse.

If *condescend* is usually a derogatory word, it is also, perhaps for that very reason, a rich and suggestive word, resonant of emotion and personality. Summoning images of arrogance and resentment, *condescend* cries to be used in novels about underdogs, especially when the underdogs overcome.

In English literature we find *condescend* in *Pride and Prejudice*, in *Frankenstein*, and in *Vanity Fair*, in *Jane Eyre* and in *Ivanhoe*, in *Wuthering Heights* and in *Silas Marner*. It was used by early masters such as Milton and Swift and by modern masters such as Conrad and Hardy.

American writers, including Fitzgerald, Crane, Melville, Ellison, and James, have also used *condescend* in their novels, and we find it both in advanced novels, such as the American classic *Moby Dick*, and in children's novels, such as the British classic *The Secret Garden*.

In the classics we find friendly condescension and affable condescension (Milton), insolent condescension (Wollstonecraft), and a princesslike condescension (Hawthorne). In *A Tale of Two Cities*, Dickens described a "grudging condescension and patronage." In Barrie's *Peter Pan*, "he would answer condescendingly."

In Swift's *Gulliver's Travels*, written in 1726, Gulliver feels gratitude to the horse-like Houyhnhnms "that they would condescend to distinguish me from the rest of my species." The noble Houyhnhnms, it seems, at first mistook Gulliver for a stupid and vulgar Yahoo. Just imagine.

In the 1792 *Vindication of the Rights of Woman*, Mary Wollstonecraft described "all the characteristics of grandeur, combined with the winning graces of condescension." She averred that women want "not the libidinous mockery of gallantry, not the insolent condescension of protectorship," and she asked men to speak to women "the language of truth and soberness, and away with the lullaby strains of condescending endearment." Strong words, even today.

In Jane Austen's *Pride and Prejudice*, the proud Lady Catherine stoops to advise her sanctimonious toady, Mr. Collins; we learn that "She had even condescended to advise him to marry as soon as he could." Collins, as we saw earlier, was breathless with such flattery. "But she is perfectly amiable," he swoons, "and often condescends to drive by my humble abode in her little phaeton and ponies." Also in *Pride and Prejudice*, Jane Austen wrote a sentence that could be easily mistaken for one by Mary Wollstonecraft: "there is meanness," she wrote, "in all the arts which ladies sometimes condescend to employ for captivation."

Condescend was used by Sir Walter Scott in *Ivanhoe*, where characters are "condescending to avail themselves of the good cheer," and it was used by Scott's contemporary James Fenimore Cooper in *The Last of the Mohicans*, where "not a hand had been extended to greet him, nor yet an eye had condescended to watch his movements."

One author who loved *condescend* was William Makepeace Thackeray, the India-born English novelist who died mercifully in 1863, before fickle history would have made his ultratraditional masterpiece, *Vanity Fair*, impossible to write. Thackeray wrote *Vanity Fair* in 1847, fourteen years before Lincoln became president; it was a time when British upper lips were still stiff and the classes still appreciated the condescension of their betters. Thackeray's characters condescend to visit, occasionally condescend to shake hands, and scarcely ever condescend to hold personal communication. Mrs. Blenkinsop, the housekeeper, Thackeray wrote, "condescended to listen on the landing-place." In *Vanity Fair*, we read that "There is no more agreeable object in life than to see Mayfair folks condescending" and that "they treated her with such extreme kindness and condescension, and patronised her so insufferably." Furthermore, "The superb Cuff himself, at whose condescension Dobbin could only blush and wonder, helped him on with his Latin verses." And we are struck by "the perfect clumsiness with which he at length condescended to take the finger which was offered for his embrace."

The Brontë sisters used *condescend* in their classic novels of heath and cliff. In Emily's *Wuthering Heights*, "she was forced to condescend to our company," and "'Shake hands, Heathcliff,' said Mr. Earnshaw condescendingly." In Charlotte's *Jane Eyre*, we read that "The equality between her and me was real; not the mere result of condescension on her part." And Jane confesses that "I did not feel insensible to his condescension, and would not seem so."

In Melville's *Moby Dick*, there is a "sort of condescending concern and compassion," and the men are addressed "in unusual terms, whether of condescension or *in terrorem*, or otherwise."

One author who had a special fondness for *condescend* was George Eliot, who used it repeatedly in her 1861 classic *Silas Marner*. In Eliot's poignant tale of the lonely old miser redeemed by a child's love, we read of "the opportunity for hectoring and condescension for their betters," of acquaintances "founded on intermittent condescension," of "the frequency with which the proud Squire condescended to preside in the parlour of the Rainbow," and of "the more select society in which Squire Cass frequently enjoyed the double pleasure of conviviality and condescension."

Eliot's subtle words revive our interest in the double edge of condescension; would convivial condescension be, as

Eliot implies, a pleasure? What pleasure would a better feel upon condescending convivially with an inferior? Pride? Smugness? Self-satisfaction at one's magnanimity? Pity? In our age when the very concept of betters and inferiors is politically incorrect, such matters are not analyzed, and we can only wonder whether banned from discussion means banned from behavior. Finally, Eliot also wrote that "there seemed to be some evidence that ghosts had a more condescending disposition than Mr. Macey attributed to them."

In 1876 in *The American*, the American Anglophile Henry James described "the only concession to self-defense that she condescended to make." Self-defense, we duly note, is beneath one. The same year, in *Tom Sawyer*, Mark Twain noted that "These two great commanders did not condescend to fight in person." Oh yeah, *those* two great commanders.

In *The Return of the Native*, Holden Caulfield's favorite book, Hardy wrote what Wildeve spoke with condescension. He also observed that "Wildeve was never asked into the house by his proud though condescending mistress." We read that "It was a condescension in me to be Clym's wife, and not a manoeuvre" and that "he even treated the wedded pair themselves with something like condescension."

Robert Louis Stevenson, the secret favorite author no one admits, used *condescend* in his wonderful novels. In *Treasure Island*, Stevenson wrote, "'Come in, Mr. Dance,' says he, very stately and condescending." In *Dr. Jekyll and Mr. Hyde*, the pitiful Dr. Jekyll explained that "this brief condescension to my evil finally destroyed the balance of my soul."

In Stephen Crane's *The Red Badge of Courage*, we read that "The latter felt immensely superior to his friend, but he inclined to condescension." The youth, Henry Fleming, marches eagerly to war, buoyed on callow fantasies of heroism. His mother's advice—*Don't try to fit the hull battle by yourself; yer jest one little feller amongst a hull lot of others*—means nothing to him. In his innocence he imagines himself to be a warrior, superior to other youths who feel afraid: "He reflected, with condescending pity: 'Too bad! Too bad! The poor devil, it makes him feel tough!'" In the end, Henry condescends no more, having run from the battle himself and having realized that Death is only death and that the world is a place for him, with green meadows, cool brooks, and soft and eternal peace. It is a moment of true enlightenment for American literature, a message of peace in a novel of war.

Although Crane's book describes the mid-nineteenth century, it was written in 1895, as modern forms of physics, warfare, and art were about to change everything, including literature, forever. Twentieth-century novels, however, would continue to employ *condescend* to describe the way we fools look down on ourselves. In Conrad's 1900 *Lord Jim*, a character "condescended to converse," for which the other characters must assuredly have been grateful.

In Kipling's 1901 *Kim*, "There would be new boys to condescend to," and "she did not condescend to look at them."

In *A Passage to India*, Forster wrote that "It is good of Mr. Fielding to condescend to visit our friend," and better, "they filed into the ramshackly room with a condescending air."

F. Scott Fitzgerald, who learned tragically that the jazziest heights are only where we fall from, used *condescend* in *The Great Gatsby*. Fitzgerald wryly satirized social pretense as "East Egg condescending to West Egg," and his character Tom Buchanan "smiled with jovial condescension."

Wilder described "a pity full of condescension" in *The Bridge of San Luis Rey*, reminding us why in our best moments we refuse to be pitied.

In *Invisible Man*, Ralph Ellison vividly depicted those "who trailed their words to us through blood and violence and ridicule and condescension with drawling smiles." Without sentiment, he observed "that world seen only as a fertile field for exploitation by Jack and his kind, and with condescension by Norton and his."

Joseph Heller, whose 1955 *Catch-22* still vibrates with prescient recency, described "a tone of respectful condescension," noted that "Aarfy replied in his most condescending manner," and wrote that "A brash assistant brought the chaplain a stolen Zippo lighter as a gift and informed him condescendingly."

Condescend sounds an ironic note in Harper Lee's *To Kill a Mockingbird*, where the precocious Scout Finch quips that "Jem condescended to take me to school the first day." Brother-sister stuff, you know. And Lee wrote that the "boy's condescension flashed to anger." Why, oh why, could Harper Lee not have been prolific like Dickens and given us a flood of novels as beautiful as this one?

What is the essence of condescension? As we see, condescension can be affable, mean, princesslike, unusual, insolent, or intermittent. It can be grudging, proud, stately, and brief. Condescension can be jovial or filled with pity. It can flash to anger. It can be respectful. We can condescend to converse, to look at someone, to visit, to reply, to watch, or to shake hands. We can condescend to listen. To govern. To excuse.

But to condescend, we must first descend. We must move from up to down, or at least view ourselves as doing so. The condescension may be based on a social class system, or it may be based on some sense of inherent superiority, but it always involves the sense of lowering oneself to another's lower level. In literature, characters who find themselves condescended to include Gulliver, Jane Eyre, Scout Finch, and that fool, Austen's Collins.

Of these, only Collins enjoys it. And in his obsequious cringing, he repels and alienates everyone around him. Regarded as an excellent marriage prospect before he arrives at the Bennet home, he is quickly rejected by all of the daughters, who find his fawning over Lady Catherine De Bourgh revolting. It is obvious to everyone but Collins himself that his slavish bootlicking is based on nothing more than a sense of servitude; he believes in the class system. For him, Lady Catherine is a "person of rank," and he is not. And in a way that he does not understand, he is half-right.

13 allude

To allude to something is to make indirect reference to it, to hint. The English verb *allude* comes to us from Latin, where we further discover the essence of the word. *Allude*, it seems, comes from the Latin *alludere*, to play with (*ad*, to; *ludere*, to play). Ah, a word with spirit. Alluding to things, rather than directly stating them, gives us a playful option: we can direct someone's attention to something without mentioning it, and he or she can recognize what is at issue without ever hearing it mentioned. Hinting and guessing. Not a bad game, that.

The question, of course, is *why*.

Why, that is, would you play such a game—of talking about what you're not talking about. Of calling attention to things that you choose not to refer to directly. What is this alluding business about, really?

Do we allude to things, rather than name them, out of courtesy? Do we allude because of fear? Do we allude from a sense of playful mischief? Do we allude from a sense of diffidence? Why, and when, would we rather not mention something than mention it?

Allude, and its noun companion *allusion*, has been a staple of English diction for centuries. Used in the seventeenth century by Milton, in the eighteenth century by Swift and Wollstonecraft, in the nineteenth century by Austen and Cooper, and in the twentieth century by Conrad and Orwell, *allude* and *allusion* have allowed writers to elude illusions. Sorry.

We find *allude* in works by John Gardner, John Knowles, and James Joyce. It was used by E.M. Forster, Thornton Wilder, and H.G. Wells. Kipling used it. Crane used it. Thomas Hardy used it, and so did Mark Twain, Henry James, and Charles Dickens. *Allude* appears prominently in novels by female authors, great authors named Jane, Charlotte, Emily, Harriet, Mary, Edith, and George. George? Austen, Brontë, Brontë, Stowe, Shelley, Wharton, and Eliot, that is.

In English and American literature, there are silly allusions, principal allusions, and allusions to smile at. There are allusions to Rousseau, and there are things that should not be alluded to, never alluded to, and far less alluded to. (Some would include Rousseau in this list.) There is, just ask Walter Scott, the prospect to which we allude. There are faint allusions and learned allusions, obscure allusions and vague allusions. There are even muttered allusions.

In *Paradise Lost*, Milton described "the walls / Of Pandemonium, City and proud seat / Of Lucifer, so by allusion call'd / Of that bright Star to Satan paragon'd." Milton finished *Paradise Lost* in 1667, and ever since critics have wondered whether Satan was actually the bright star of the poem. It could be; he certainly has a James-Dean-wounded-charisma aura, as he plummets in defeat to painful Hell from the plains of Heaven and flies across Chaos to get God back by messing up the Divine plans for the stupid blue planet.

Swift's gullible Gulliver has to "show my wit by a silly allusion," but the ingenuous Gulliver, having little wit to show in 1726, was probably wasting his time.

Mary Wollstonecraft, who had wit and more, wrote, "I do not mean to allude to the romantic passion, which is the concomitant of genius." Readers, take note, and encourage those romantic (as in *Romantic era*) passions for learning that obsess bright children. Virtually every great creative mind was encouraged in early passions by a mentor. Yes, romantic passion is the concomitant of genius.

In *Pride and Prejudice*, Jane Austen described "subjects, which her sisters would not have alluded to for the world."

Mary Shelley loved *allude*. In *Frankenstein*, she wrote, "You will smile at my allusion," and "every word that I spoke in allusion to it caused my lips to quiver, and my heart to palpitate." Rarely, except in brilliant novels, do allusions give us quivering lips, though palpitating hearts are a different matter. Shelley also wrote, "But until then, I conjure you, do not mention it or allude to it."

James Fenimore Cooper's characters allude at will. We read that "David smiled sadly, though not without a momentary gleam of pleasure, at this allusion to his beloved vocation." Then, "when he alluded to their injuries, their eyes kindled with fury." One Cooper character reacts "as if recalled to such a recollection by the allusion to the massacre." And another knows what's up, "though nothing present assisted him in discovering the object of their allusion." Allusions can hint at most anything: "I understand not," a Cooper character states, "your allusions about line and angles.'"

Thackeray, in *Vanity Fair*, used *allude* to reveal the affected disingenuousness of Becky Sharp: "When Miss Sharp was agitated, and alluded to her maternal relatives, she spoke with ever so slight a foreign accent, which gave a great charm to her clear ringing voice." This, in spite of the fact that ordinarily, "The humble calling of her female parent Miss Sharp never alluded to." We should think not.

In Charlotte Brontë's *Jane Eyre*, one is "never troubled or startled by one noxious allusion." Dear us, no; noxious allusions are not to be endured. We also read that "no new allusion was made to the subject over which I brooded."

In Charlotte's sister Emily's novel, the Catherine and Heathcliff thing, there is an "allusion to my morning's speech." Those who think that intelligence has no genetic component can ponder the novels of the Brontës and be amazed.

Hawthorne, in *The House of the Seven Gables*, wrote that Hepzibah was "not displeased at this allusion to the somber dignity of an inherited curse." An inherited curse, of course, is one somber dignity that most of us could do without. Sanguine dignities, we prefer.

In Harriet Beecher Stowe's *Uncle Tom's Cabin*, there is "the least allusion to my ill health," but "he has never alluded to the subject since." Furthermore, there are definite occurrences "whenever her husband's or Eva's wishes with regard to the servants were alluded to."

Melville's story of the great white whale, *Moby Dick*, contains "a thorough appreciative understanding of the more special leviathanic revelations and allusions of all sorts." Melville wrote that "such a nomenclature may be convenient in facilitating allusions to some kinds of whales," and we find that "By some tacit consent, throughout the voyage little or no allusion was made to it, especially by the mates." In fact, "allusion has only been made to whatever way-side, antecedent, extra prospects were his."

In *A Tale of Two Cities*, Charles Dickens described an "incidental allusion, purposely thrown out." And in *Silas Marner*, George Eliot wrote that "it was already four years since there had been any allusion to the subject between them." Eliot noted that "Dolly was too useful a woman not to have many opportunities of illumination of the kind she alluded to."

Henry James used *allude* frequently. In *The American*, he described "a devotee of something mysterious and sacred to which he occasionally alluded" and observed that "no such allusions should be made." He noted that "she made no allusion to the circumstances under which he had been presented to her" and described "the smile with which he had greeted Newman's allusion to his promised request." Knowingly, James described how, "failing to gather any satisfaction from his allusions, she at last directly inquired" and wrote that "He irritated our friend by the tone of his allusions to their native country." Finally, James captured the supercilious aura of European society in describing the "atmosphere…purified by allusions of a thoroughly superior cast."

In Mark Twain's *Tom Sawyer*, we learn that, "if he had any dim idea of making any 'references to allusions,' he thought better of it."

And in Robert Louis Stevenson's *Dr. Jekyll and Mr. Hyde*, a character pleads, "I beg that you will spare me any allusion to one whom I regard as dead."

In *The Red Badge of Courage*, Stephen Crane described "profane allusions to a general," and he must have had difficulty wiping that smile off his authorial face.

Thomas Hardy used *allude* in his *fin de siècle* novels of English England. In *The Return of the Native*, he described "the particular sound alluded to," and in *The Mayor of Casterbridge*, wherein our drunken hero sells his wife, "mother inadvertently alluded to her favourite's movements."

In *The War of the Worlds*, H.G. Wells's anonymous narrator narrates that he "may allude here to the curious suggestions of the red weed."

In Kipling's *Kim*, we read that "*Lear* was not so full of historical allusions as *Julius Caesar*."

Joseph Conrad, in *Lord Jim*, described "Some muttered allusions, which followed, to dogs and the smell of roast-meat." Good dogs might object to their allusions being muttered, we fear. Conrad observed things "coming to the surface of the most distant allusions" and had a character say, "I knew very well he was not alluding to his duties." "From his allusions," Conrad wrote, "I understand she had been an educated...girl." In *Heart of Darkness*, Conrad wrote, "What we afterwards alluded to as an attack was really an attempt at repulse." A character in *Heart of Darkness* is seen "alluding with a toss of the head to the tumult in the station yard," and another complains, "He alluded constantly to Europe, to the people I was supposed to know there." Another character "was invariably alluded to as 'that scoundrel.'"

Surely the most charming of all *allude* sentences comes from Kenneth Grahame in *The Wind in the Willows*. In his tale of Ratty, and Badger, and Mole, and of course the incorrigible Toad, Grahame explains that "it is quite against animal-etiquette to dwell on possible trouble ahead, or even to allude to it." Sweet, furry optimists.

In Edith Wharton's *Ethan Frome*, we read that "Ethan had imagined that his allusion might open the way to the accepted pleasantries" and that he found himself "fearing he hardly knew what: criticism, complaints, or vague allusions to the imminent probability of her marrying."

James Joyce, who led modern authors deep into the interior of the human personality, began with a semi-fictionalized portrait of himself as a young man, cryptically entitled *A Portrait of the Artist as a Young Man*. In this portrait, Joyce, or should we say James, or should we say Stephen, observed that "Any allusion made to his father by a fellow or by a master put his calm to rout in a moment." He also described the "tiny flame which the priest's allusion had kindled upon Stephen's cheek."

Forster's *A Passage to India* concerns several passages, the one to India being probably the least significant, although it depends which India one means: the geographical India, the cultural India, or the spiritual India. In one passage from *A Passage*, "They attacked one another with obscure allusions and had a silly quarrel," and in another, "Her remarks pleased him, but his mind shut up tight because she had alluded to her marriage." We read that "this story of her private failure she dared not allude to."

In Thornton Wilder's *The Bridge of San Luis Rey*, "Only the faintest allusion to them occurs in the Correspondence." A character "presently began improvising couplets alluding to her appearance," and we discover "All those allusions to honour, reputation, and the flame of love, all the metaphors about birds."

Joseph Heller used *allusion* in his oblique *Catch-22*, observing that "The vast majority consisted of allusions to prior communications which Major Major had never seen or heard of." Although his sentence ends with a dreaded preposition, we still describe Heller as an author, an author who also wrote that "General Peckem chuckled with jaunty relish and sailed smoothly along toward a favorite learned allusion." General Peckem. Somewhere, in a too-neglected grave, the soily remains of Stephen Crane are chuckling mirthfully at the mind of Joseph Heller.

From John Knowles's *A Separate Peace*, we lift the following specimen: "He alluded to last night only by asking how Phineas was." And even from John Gardner's *Grendel*, we can learn that "'Back there in Time' is an allusion of language."

In these three centuries of examples, ranging from John Milton in 1667 to John Gardner in 1989, is there an answer to our question: Why do we allude to things, rather than directly refer to them?

It is perhaps useful to notice what an allusion does not do: it does not conceal. It isn't that by alluding we intend to conceal from another what we are making reference to; on the contrary, both direct reference and indirect allusion are means of reference that are understood by both parties in a communication. That is why we find sentences such as Joyce's, in which any "allusion to his father by a fellow or by a master put his calm to rout in a moment." The allusion may be indirect rather than direct, but the message is still delivered. Or consider Forster's passage: "They attacked one another with obscure allusions and had a silly quarrel." There would hardly be a silly quarrel over allusions whose references were not noticed.

And so allusions are not for things to which we dare not refer; they are for things to which we dare not refer *directly*. Indeed, our survey of literary sentences makes clear that there is a category of things to which we must neither refer nor allude. Recall Jane Austen's "subjects, which her sisters would not have alluded to for the world." And from Mary Shelley, we got the sentence, "But until then, I conjure you, do not mention it or allude to it." And Stevenson wrote, "I beg that you will spare me any allusion to one whom I regard as dead," although that sentence was itself an example of the allusion that it was forbidding. Hmmm. And remember Grahame's lovely explanation of animal etiquette, in which possible trouble ahead is neither to be mentioned nor even alluded to. Animals have more sense.

On the other hand, what *do* we allude to? To the romantic passion, remember? To a morning's speech. To a beloved vocation. To the somber dignity of an inherited curse. To ill health. To something mysterious and sacred. To that scoundrel. To one's father. To her appearance. To last night. To the imminent probability of her marrying.

Perhaps the allusion may often be best understood as an invitation, as a way of putting the ball in the other fellow's court. Feeling uncomfortable about mentioning something ourselves, we become circumspect and float the subject past discreetly. If you want to talk about this, the allusion means, we can.

That, of course, implies a certain benevolence on the part of the speaker. If malevolence is present, then the allusion can be hostile, intended to hurt or embarrass or to parade a cruel subject in front of witnesses while maintaining a sanctimonious denial that such was ever one's meaning. That might be an allusion such as the one Dickens described: "an incidental allusion, purposefully thrown out."

A complex subject.

Allusions, it would appear, are yet another manifestation of the profundity and complexity of the human mind. A chronic manifestation.

That would explain why our novels, like our lives, are filled with allusions. *Good* novels, I mean, if you know the ones to which I allude.

14 odious

Odious is one of the strong words in the commodious English language. Being only a slight variation of the Latin *odiosus*, which to the tramping Roman legions meant hateful, *odious* survives as an adjective for what is especially detestable, despicable, hateful, offensive, repugnant, or disgusting. *Odious* is the adjective form of the noun *odium*, which is the state of contempt, discredit, opprobrium, infamy, disrepute, or condemnation that we reserve for what is odious.

It is always worth remembering that etymology is a kind of archaeology of the mind, or perhaps of the mouth. *Odious*, like many words in our English, is a relic, a cultural artifact that we complacently mouth in an unconscious imitation of unknown ancestors from lost civilizations. In the case of *odious*, the ancestors were Romans, who undoubtedly thought that the barbarian Gauls were *odiosus*, but then, the Gauls probably appreciated Rome's invasion of their green heartland less than we can imagine.

Two thousand years from now, will there be a civilization in North America that speaks a future form of the Latin *odiosus*? Will they speak a descendant of our language that we would be unable to understand, just as the Romans would not understand our English? Will they refer to what they despise as *odee*, or *odo*, or *otos*? Will they be as interested in us as we are in the ancient Romans, who lived two thousand years before our time? Will they dig carefully in our ruins, and will a future Gibbon tell our story and write translations of our classics?

Of course, it is difficult to imagine that our own civilization and language could ever vanish; we seem so permanent to ourselves. But considering how our culture and language have changed—changed utterly, Yeats would say—in only four decades, it must be imagined that things would be virtually unrecognizable in twenty centuries.

In English and American literature of the last four centuries, we find continual use of *odious*; from Shakespeare to Joseph Heller, writers have used *odious* to describe our repugnance for what we detest. And we detest many things.

We detest odious faces, odious truths, and odious insects. We detest odious people and their odious habits. We detest odious attitudes.

In *The Tempest*, Shakespeare wrote, "This my mean task / Would be as heavy to me as odious, but / The mistress which I serve quickens what's dead / And makes my labors pleasures."

That was in 1611. Fifty-six years later Milton wrote *Paradise Lost*—he said—to justify the ways of God to man. Milton's biography shows that he may have had some difficulty justifying the ways of God, since his efforts to contribute to civilization met with the neat combination of political persecution, imprisonment, and blindness, not to mention that his own daughters found him so odious that they only regretted that news of his third marriage was not news of his death. Milton's paradise was lost, indeed. In his good book, though, we find poem-characters who burn odious offerings, who have odious offspring, and who hear the "odious din of War." There is odious truth, as well as these words from Adam as he decides to accompany Eve out of paradise: "For bliss, as thou has part, to me is bliss, / Tedious, unshar'd with thee, and odious soon."

Jonathan Swift, who wrote *Gulliver's Travels* in 1726, apparently found it more difficult to justify the ways of man to man. In his scathing classic satire, he placed Gulliver in every absurd situation that a credulous dupe could be in. Gulliver finds "odious insects, each of them as big as a Dunstable lark." He is seen "daubing my face and clothes with its odious slime" and abhors "the squeezes given me by this odious animal." Eventually, Gulliver himself is mistaken for a filthy Yahoo: "I expressed my uneasiness at his giving me so often the appellation of Yahoo, an odious animal for which I had so utter a hatred and contempt." Even today, Swift would not be surprised to learn, odious Yahoos are all too common.

In Jane Austen's *Pride and Prejudice*, written in 1813, we read that the "sight of Miss Lucas was odious to her," and Mrs. Bennet is heard to remark, "Pray do not talk to that odious man."

In Mary Shelley's 1816 *Frankenstein*, Victor Frankenstein describes "the room which had been the scene of my odious work." Later, he "looks upon study as an odious fetter." There is an "odious companion," and the monster moans that "the minutest description of my odious and loathsome person is given, in language which painted your own horrors." Poor monster. How sad to have an odious and loathsome person, especially when referring to the person who one *is*.

In Sir Walter Scott's *Ivanhoe*, "The sight of Front-de-Boeuf himself is less odious to me than thou."

Thackeray loved *odious*. Of course, Thackeray loved many words, but *odious* is especially prominent in his 1847 *Vanity Fair*. Therein, Thackeray described "the old iron carved doors, which are something like those at odious Chiswick" and "the house of Queen's Crawley, which is an odious old-fashioned red brick mansion." In *Vanity Fair*, there is "your dear muslin gown (about which that odious

Mrs. Pinner was so rude, because you gave it me)." We read that a "stranger was administering her medicines—a stranger from the country—an odious Miss...." There is a "little odious governess," and "As for going back to that odious brother of mine after what has passed, it is out of the question." With bated breath, we read that "he might urge her to do her duty, and cast off that odious reprobate who has disgraced himself and his family." And we learn that "You shall leave that odious regiment: quit gaming, racing, and be a good boy." Of course, becoming a good boy is no small feat, especially when one has a proclivity for gaming and racing, and even more so within the jaded pages of *Vanity Fair*.

In Emily Brontë's 1847 *Wuthering Heights*, we find "his staunch supporter, that odious old man," and we "behold that odious Joseph standing, rubbing his bony hands, and quivering." But it is Heathcliff who steals the scene with his saturnine thunder: "I hate them all," he storms, "they are odious beings."

Emily's sister Charlotte, in her also-1847 *Jane Eyre*, wrote that "that recollection was then, and is now, inexpressibly odious to me."

Nathaniel Hawthorne used *odious* in his novels of conscience. In *The Scarlet Letter*, "His gestures...were odious in the clergyman's sight." In *The House of the Seven Gables*, there is "an odious picture on the wall," and we read that the "house, in my view, is expressive of that odious and abominable Past, with all its bad influences, against which I have just been declaiming." And there is a question: "Will he bear about with him no odious grin of feigned benignity, insolent in its pretense, and loathsome in its falsehood?"

Hawthorne's friend Melville used *odious* in *Moby Dick* to ask, "Now how did this odious stigma originate?"

In *Silas Marner*, George Eliot described an unhappy woman "whose image became more odious to him every day." And she observed that "the revelation might be made even in a more odious way than by Dunstan's malignity."

Henry James, whom William Faulkner described as "one of the nicest old ladies I ever met," loved the word *odious* and used it repeatedly in his Europhilic novels. In *The American*, James described "an odious old gentleman" and a woman who "seemed an odious blot upon the face of nature." Newman, James's American, has "been odiously successful." In a quintessence—or would it be a nonpareil, or would it be a paragon?—of ambivalence, James's character Mrs. Tristram exclaims, "'I think it is odious!' ...And then in a moment: 'I think it is delicious!'" Odiously delicious, perhaps. One character shows "her perfect comprehension of his finding her conduct odious," and another confesses, "It would be quite odious for me to come talking to you as if I could patronise you."

Another American, the newman Mark Twain, whose real name was Sam, wrote in *Tom Sawyer* that the experience of temporary freedom "made the going into captivity and fetters again so much more odious."

In *Treasure Island*, Stevenson described the "case of natives, buccaneers, or the odious French." And in his *Dr. Jekyll and Mr. Hyde*, he observed that "A flash of odious joy appeared upon the woman's face."

In 1900 Joseph Conrad, who became a classic author in his second language, wrote *Lord Jim*, where he described "an odious and fleshy figure" and observed a character "lying extended on his back in a cane chair, odiously unbuttoned." "That's how he looked," Conrad wrote, "and it was odious." In *Lord Jim*, the "perforated pipe gurgled, choked, spat, and splashed in odious ridicule of a swimmer fighting for his life." Conrad also noted that "the blunder was of an odious, of an unfortunate nature." In Conrad's darkhearted *Heart of Darkness*, it was "as if something altogether monstrous, intolerable to thought and odious to the soul" existed.

In his 1924 novel *A Passage to India*, E.M. Forster wrote that "Here was Aziz all shoddy and odious."

In Orwell's 1949 *1984*, "there was only the odious scarlet sash."

Perhaps *odious* sounds slightly outmoded, a dated word that has lost its luster? Perhaps it sounds too nineteenth century? Perhaps it has too British a stilted superciliousness? Well, no. In his too modern, too American, too delicious *Catch-22*, no less an America ruffian than Joseph Heller described a character who had "been busted right down to private for making odious audible comparisons about the commissioned officers for whom he worked." Well, audible comparisons *are* odious, and we must thank Joseph Heller for pointing that out. In *Catch-22*, even a name can be odious: "It was an odious, alien, distasteful name, a name that just did not inspire confidence." We read that something "really is odious and certainly will offend your conscience," and we watch as characters draw "back with terror and revulsion, as though trying to shrink away from their own odious skins."

In 1977 American Nobel Laureate Toni Morrison used *odious* in *Song of Solomon*: "The image left him," she wrote, "but the odiousness never did."

What does it signify, this adjective *odious*? We can see that its noun parent, *odium*, is used less frequently, although it may retain more impact as a result. But *odious* packs, as the cliché says, a wallop. Part of its walloppackingness is in its sound. *Odious* sounds odious; it sounds like *odor*, although that word traces through the Latin *odor* to the Greek *ozein*, to smell. Do not talk, says Mrs. Bennet, to that odious man. Something in the sound, something in the strength of the first-syllable stress, *O dee uss*, something in the music of the Latinate English resonates with our sense of contempt and repulsion. *O dee uss.* How odious. That odious man. That odious Joseph, rubbing his bony hands and quivering. Something odious to the soul. Here was Aziz, all shoddy and odious.

Odious. Eww. How odious, alien, and distasteful. Odious. Odious audible comparisons. Odiously unbuttoned. Odious and fleshy. A flash of odious joy. The odious French.

Somehow, *odious* communicates something more repulsive than *hateful*. We would rather, we sense, be hateful any day than odious. We want everyone not to regard us as odious beings, as having an odious face, odious manners, or an odious grin. We want not to be branded by an odious stigma. We do not want the sight of us to be odious to others; we do not want to be compared to odious slime, odious Yahoos, or odious reprobates.

What accounts for the power of *odious*? It is some combination of song and psychology, a music of repulsion that resonates with our emotional being. For we are, after all, emotional beings who sense and respond, like and dislike, love and detest. And somewhere beyond the terrain of ordinary emotions, the mild reactions of our mundane lives, there is the memorable zone of extreme detestation, of repulsion that is revolting, of disgust that makes our skin crawl. Not pleasant, but not readily forgotten. In its own way, the feeling that something is odious is a peak of experience. It signifies that we are alive, reacting and choosing.

Odious, to us, are those things we find most offensive: crudeness that emphasizes base animal realities, cruelty and indifference that disregard the required caring of civilized mentality, visible ugliness that insults our delight in the physical world, needless reminders of our ephemeral nature, gross egocentrism, vulgar inattention to personal standards of dress or speech or courtesy. Odious, to us, are those things that diminish what we love most, what we prize most highly.

Look closely, and odious essence of *odious* is visible: "Will he bear about with him," asked Hawthorne, "no odious grin of feigned benignity?" There, there, you see? The odious grin of feigned benignity. The odious grin. Of *feigned* benignity.

Despicable...despicable. *O dee uss.*

Men should be, Iago said, what they seem. But when it comes to benignity, we should, like Hamlet, know not seems. To feign benignity, the tender quality that most expresses the human side of human nature, is odious, but perhaps doing so is what expresses the inhuman side of our ambiguous, paradoxical, human nature. It is, we think, an odious ambiguity.

15placid

The peaceful English adjective *placid* means tranquil, calm, untroubled. We are pleased by the quiet and undisturbed feeling of a placid environment or a placid mind, and this is to be expected, since *placid* comes to us from the Romans' word *placidus*, a relative of *placere*, to please. *Placid* has expectable variations such as *placidly* and *placidity*, but it also has subtle word connections that may go unnoticed; when we placate others, we make them placid, unless they are implacable.

Placid is another classic word, a friend of the mind that has been in heavy employ by British and American authors for centuries. *Placid* has been used by modern writers such as Sylvia Plath and Pearl Buck, by nineteenth-century writers such as George Eliot, Harriet Beecher Stowe, and Charlotte Brontë, and by eighteenth-century writers such as Mary Wollstonecraft.

In our literature, there are placid lakes, placid expressions, and placid remarks. The sun can be placid, as can a son.

Of course, Mary Wollstonecraft is remembered not for her son but for her daughter, Mary Shelley, who wrote a monstrous novel. In Mary Wollstonecraft's 1792 treatise *Vindication of the Rights of Woman*, she described "the placid satisfaction that unsophisticated affections impart" and noted how someone had "invited with placid fervor the mild reflection of her sister's beams to turn to her chaste bosom."

Mary's daughter Mary wrote *Frankenstein* in 1816, before the Civil War introduced the industrial revolution to the process of human destruction and an author could still drift in the not-so-placid waves of Romanticism. In *Frankenstein*, there is a placid home, but with a message: "our placid home, and our contented hearts are regulated by the same immutable laws." On the lake, "the waters were placid." In fact, "the sky and lake are blue and placid," and "the way was smooth and placid as a southern sea." Shelley described how "the lovely Isis, which flows beside it through meadows of exquisite verdure, is spread forth into a placid expanse of waters." And Victor Frankenstein describes how his bride-to-be "looked forward to our union with placid contentment."

In Sir Walter Scott's *Ivanhoe*, we learn that Cedric "was in no very placid state of mind," and in James Fenimore Cooper's *The Last of the Mohicans*, there is "a rifle, whose ball came skipping along the placid surface of the strait."

The year 1847 was a good one for *placid*, which found itself being used in three immortal novels: *Jane Eyre*, *Wuthering Heights*, and *Vanity Fair*. In *Vanity Fair*, Thackeray described Miss Crawley, "who was placidly occupied with a French novel." In *Wuthering Heights*, Emily Brontë described how Catherine "endured his efforts placidly." And in Charlotte Brontë's novel of indomitable character, Jane Eyre found that her temper could be stroked and smoothed "into placidity."

In Nathaniel Hawthorne's *The Scarlet Letter*, the child Pearl "lay in the placidity of sleep," which must be the only placidity to be had in that anxiety-ridden novel.

Harriet Beecher Stowe used *placid* in her tirade against the cruelty of slavery, *Uncle Tom's Cabin*. She described "the plain white muslin handkerchief, lying in placid folds across her bosom." Placid handkerchief folds are one thing, but Stowe also used *placid* to describe the personality: "he found the placid, sunny temper, which had been the habitude of his life, broken in on." We hate it when the habitudes of our lives are broken in on, do we not? Poetically, Stowe described "a high placid forehead, on which time had written no inscription."

In 1851, the same year that Stowe's *Uncle Tom's Cabin* burst upon the world, Melville published *Moby Dick*, a mystic and at times almost hallucinatory novel that continues to haunt our imaginations with images of Starbuck, Ishmael, Ahab, and Queequeg. Of the sperm whale, Melville wrote, "I think his broad brow to be full of a prairie-like placidity, born of a speculative indifference as to death." Ah, those speculative whales.

In Charles Dickens's *A Tale of Two Cities*, "the sun rose bright, placid, and beautiful," and "Miss Ross inquired, with placidity."

George Eliot used *placid* in her 1861 novel of lonely humanity redeemed through love, *Silas Marner*. In *Silas Marner*, there is the "firm yet placid mouth, the clear veracious glance of the brown eyes." There is "the placid churchyard with the long shadows of the gravestones across the bright green hillocks." And there is "Dolly, who sat with a placid listening face, now bordered by grey hairs." The good value of a placid listening face, we consider, is underestimated.

In *The American*, Henry James explained that "It was not an excitement or perplexity; it was a placid, fathomless sense of diversion." In *The American*, "He reflected with sober placidity" and "allowed his placid eyes to measure his friend's generous longitude."

In his inimitable prose, Thomas Hardy used *placid* in *The Return of the Native*. He described "the end of the four or five years of endeavour which follow the close of placid pupilage" and noted that "We can hardly imagine bucolic placidity quickening to intellectual aims without imagining social aims as the transitional phase." Ah, let us again recall the close of our placid pupilage and the quickening of our bucolic placidity. Hardy also used *placid* in *The Mayor of Casterbridge* to describe the effect of "disturbing the minds of the placid burgesses" and to observe that there "may, too, have been enough recklessness and resentment beneath her ordinary placidity to make her stifle any momentary doubts."

In Stevenson's *Treasure Island*, we see "Silver himself, standing placidly by." Placidly, yes, but not innocently. In Wilde's *The Picture of Dorian Gray*, Dorian answered his mother "with a placid expression in her face." In Kipling's *Kim*, there is a "scowl at the placid old man in the corner." And in Stephen Crane's *The Red Badge of Courage*, young Henry Fleming's fear of death changes his view of everything: "A house standing placidly in distant fields had to him an ominous look."

One author who loved *placid* was Joseph Conrad. Writing at the turn of the century, Conrad published *Lord Jim* in 1900 and *Heart of Darkness* in 1902. In *Lord Jim*, Conrad described "the placid tenderness of a mother's face," the "courteous placidity that argued an immense power of self-control," a "thoughtful placid face" that twitched once, and "his caustic placidity." In *Heart of Darkness*, "We felt meditative, and fit for nothing but placid staring." According to Conrad, the "manager was very placid," and "the swift and indifferent placidity of that look troubled me."

Barrie's *Peter Pan* takes us on a flight of imagination from which we never, never land. The characters of Hook, Peter, Tinker Bell, Smee, and Wendy become inhabitants of our internal world. In *Peter Pan*, Mrs. Darling was placid, "John continued to sleep so placidly on the floor," and Smee "was hemming placidly." Ah, hem.

In Kenneth Grahame's softly titled *The Wind in the Willows*, there is a face with a "placid, satisfied expression," "the Badger only remarked placidly," and the lakes "lay so blue and placid below me."

In Edith Wharton's 1911 *Ethan Frome*, there is "a shake of the reins that sent the sorrel placidly jogging down the hill."

In *The Good Earth*, Pearl Buck described "a fat, placid child" and wrote that "the waters lay placid and unmoved except for the slight summer wind that rose at sunset."

Richard Wright used *placid* in *Native Son* to describe how "the white cat bounded past him and leaped upon the desk; it sat looking at him with large placid eyes and mewed plaintively." Wright wrote that "Bigger's eyes were wide and placid, gazing into space."

In 1952 Ernest Hemingway described an old man at sea hooked to a fish bigger than his boat. Aren't we all? Hooked to a fish bigger than our boat, I mean. Hemingway's old man, Santiago, should have cut the fish loose, but he wouldn't do it. Couldn't do it. It was a matter of principle, and anyway, on "each calm placid turn the fish made he was gaining line."

In Arthur Miller's *The Crucible*, "Cheever waits placidly, the sublime official, dutiful."

In Joseph Heller's *Catch-22*, there is a placid blue sea, placid interest, and "Aarfy, who had struck a match and was placidly lighting his pipe."

We find *placid* in Neville Shute's *On the Beach*: "Kind of placid, I'd say," in Sylvia Plath's *The Bell Jar*: "I woke warm and placid in my white cocoon," and in Harper Lee's *To Kill a Mockingbird*, where Jem speaks placidly and where it "had been a placid week."

In *Song of Solomon*, Toni Morrison used *placid* with chilling effect: "Inside the cave the dead man was still looking placidly up at him, but the tarpaulin and the gold were gone."

Placid. Once again, we find a word that has itself become a classic, a word that fills the need we have to express life through language. For centuries, authors have used this good word to indicate what is calm and untroubled, and we find them describing not just what is literally placid, such as placid seas, placid waters, placid skies, placid churchyards, and placid sleep, but also what is metaphorically placid. The greatest writers have a way of surprising our expectations of usage, of finding turns of expression that our dictionary-level assumptions of *placid* would never predict. Toni Morrison described a dead man as looking placidly up, leaving us caught on the point of contradiction. Joseph Conrad discovered a caustic placidity, leaving us to resolve the paradox ourselves. Thomas Hardy could bind the world in the nutshell of a phrase, such as his descriptions of placid pupilage and bucolic placidity. Harriet Beecher Stowe could find placidity in the folds of a handkerchief, though we'd never have thought of that ourselves. Sometimes placidity is good, as in Dickens's sun rising placid and beautiful, and sometimes placidity is bad, as in the minds of Hardy's placid burgesses. Sometimes *placid* indicates something low, as when Mary Wollstonecraft observed "the placid satisfaction that unsophisticated affections impart," and sometimes *placid* indicates something high, as when Thackeray described Miss Crawley placidly occupied with a French novel. Sometimes *placid* hits us with delayed effect, as when Sylvia Plath has Esther Greenwood say, "I woke warm and placid in my white cocoon," and we realize in the afterimage that she is describing the effect of fading anesthesia after a suicide attempt.

Sometimes we wonder at the subtlety of a phrase. What, exactly, did George Eliot mean by a firm yet placid mouth?

What did Mary Wollstonecraft mean by the apparent oxymoron *placid fervour*? What did Edith Wharton intend to suggest by describing her sorrel as placidly jogging? What did Harriet Beecher Stowe mean by a high, placid forehead? And what did Melville mean by describing the whale brow as "full of a prairie-like placidity, born of a speculative indifference as to death"?

Calm.

We sleep placidly, endure placidly, stand placidly, remark placidly, wait placidly, gaze placidly, reflect placidly, read placidly, and listen placidly.

We have placid homes, placid tempers, placid surfaces, placid expanses, placid expressions, placid eyes, placid turns, placid satisfactions, and placid interests.

And then we have all of the experiences in life that are not placid, that are anything but placid, but for those, we must use another word.

16 incredulous

The dubious adjective *incredulous*, meaning full of disbelief, reached the English language from the shores of Italy. Like the majority of other classic words in English, *incredulous* comes from ancient Latin, where it lived its Roman incarnation as the word *incredulus*. In two thousand years, we have added an *o* to the word. Well, if it ain't broke, they say, don't fix it.

Incredulous ain't broke.

Yes, I know that we lovers of language are supposed to regard *ain't* as substandard, to be avoided by anyone not wishing to be considered illiterate. And I know that *broke* should be *broken*.

But rules were made to be broke.

I'll give you a second to recover.

Apoplexy hurts.

All right. *If it is not broken, then do not fix it, and rules were made to be broken.*

Now, back to *incredulous*.

Incredulous came to English with its family: *credulous, credulity, incredulity, credible, incredible*, and more distant relatives such as *credit, creditable, credo, discredit, creed*, and even *miscreant*. *Cred*, that's the thing: belief. A credulous person believes too easily and is victim to credulity, when he, or possibly she, should show more incredulity. A story is credible when one may believe it, and incredible when one cannot. Credit is based on belief, a credo is a belief, and one has been discredited when others' belief in her, or possibly him, has been lost. A creed is a belief system, and a miscreant is a villainous misbeliever.

Incredulous is often mistaken for its start-alike *incredible*—a rank mistake if ever there was one. Something is incredible if it is difficult to believe; the person who then disbelieves the incredible is said to be incredulous. It is *it* that is incredible and *we* who are incredulous.

In *Cyrano de Bergerac*, Christian is incredulous when he first sees Cyrano's incredible, protruberant nose. "Oh no," he cries. "Impossible! Exaggerated!" It is a moment of literary incredulity that makes us laugh.

Incredulous often appears in its adverb guise, *incredulously*, and sometimes in its noun guise, *incredulity*.

Curiously, *incredulous* seems to have come into widespread usage in later centuries, compared to other classic words. Even the *Oxford English Dictionary*, which typically traces words from the thirteenth century, gives no examples of usage before the late 1500s, and the first example of *incredulous* in my classic words study is from Jane Austen's *Pride and Prejudice*, written in 1813. *Incredulous*, then, has a modern face; it is a friend of Orwell, Miller, Golding, Heller, Knowles, and Morrison. Perhaps the unexpected modern world has generated more incredulity than the past could equal; that would surprise no one.

In Jane Austen's *Pride and Prejudice*, we find an "audience not merely wondering, but incredulous." Austen described how "Elizabeth looked at her sister with incredulous solicitude" and wrote that Darcy looked up "with a smile of affected incredulity." Of course, one must be quite sophisticated to *affect* incredulity, must not one? Austen wrote that, though "suspicion was very far from Miss

Bennet's general habits, she was absolutely incredulous here."

In Mary Shelley's classic *Frankenstein*, she wrote, "I believe I left him incredulous to the last." Furthermore, the magistrate "appeared at first perfectly incredulous," and "the whole tide of his incredulity returned."

In James Fenimore Cooper's *The Last of the Mohicans*, "Magua shook his head incredulously," and one character "cast an incredulous look at his features." Incredulous looks at our features can, of course, be disconcerting.

In Thackeray's *Vanity Fair*, "little Osborne, gasping and in tears, looked up with wonder and incredulity at seeing this amazing champion put up suddenly to defend him."

The Brontës used *incredulous* frequently. In Emily Brontë's *Wuthering Heights*, we learn that "You may look incredulous, if you please!" And much of the time, we do please. And in Charlotte Brontë's *Jane Eyre*, she described how "incredulity and delight were expressed by her looks and gestures." Jane, we read, finds Mr. Rochester "looking darkly and doubtfully on my face, as incredulous of my sanity." And later, she smiles incredulously.

In Hawthorne's *The Scarlet Letter*, he wrote that "perhaps there was more truth in the rumor than our modern incredulity may be inclined to admit." That was in 1847, but there it is already: our modern incredulity. This modern incredulity, yes, has increased considerably in the century and a half since Hawthorne's day, but is perhaps threatened by our modern cynicism. It is becoming difficult to become sufficiently surprised.

Harriet Beecher Stowe used *incredulous* in *Uncle Tom's Cabin* to explain that "the ear that has never heard anything but abuse is strangely incredulous of anything so heavenly as kindness" and to describe "the entire incredulity with which she had met Eliza's suspicions." Vividly, Stowe wrote that

"Topsy gave the short, blunt laugh that was her common mode of expressing incredulity."

The most incredible novel of American literature, *Moby Dick*, is rich with Herman Melville's use of *incredulous*. Melville wrote that "there was a wondering gaze of incredulous curiosity in his countenance" and described the "incredulity which a profound ignorance of the entire subject may induce in some minds." The "incredulous captain," Melville wrote, "would fain have been rid of him." In *Moby Dick*, "that man held up that picture, and exhibited that stump to an incredulous world," and we learn that it is natural "to be somewhat incredulous concerning the populousness of the more enormous creatures of the globe," although we also read, "I trust you will have renounced all ignorant incredulity." Having read Melville, we suspect that there was a wondering gaze of incredulous curiosity in his own countenance, enabling him to write such a phrase.

Many other authors have used *incredulous* to describe our surprised reactions to the incredible. Thoreau noted that "my friends used to listen with incredulity when I told them." In *The American*, Henry James noted "an almost touching incredulity," and in *The Mayor of Casterbridge*, Thomas Hardy wrote that "she could see that Farfrae was still incredulous." In *Dr. Jekyll and Mr. Hyde*, Robert Louis Stevenson wrote, "and yet I shall die incredulous," and H.G. Wells, in *The Time Machine*, described how "we all followed him, puzzled but incredulous." Joseph Conrad wrote in *Lord Jim* that "I was overwhelmed by a slow incredulous amazement." And in *Kim*, Rudyard Kipling described characters "urging some scheme on Mr. Bennett, who seemed incredulous." In Kenneth Grahame's immortal *The Wind in the Willows*, we find "the astonished and hitherto incredulous Mole." In *The Secret Garden*, Burnett wrote, "'Tha' doesn't want thy porridge!' Martha exclaimed incredulously." E.M. Forster used *incredulous* in *A Passage to India*, in which "McBryde gave a faint, incredulous smile, and started rummaging in the drawer." And Edith Wharton, in *Ethan Frome*, described how "Frome heard the girl's voice, gaily incredulous" and how "Ethan's incredulity escaped in a short laugh."

An author who particularly loved *incredulous* was the perhaps too credulous F. Scott Fitzgerald. In *The Great Gatsby*, written in 1925, Fitzgerald wrote that "Her host looked at her incredulously." He described Tom Buchanan's voice as "incredulous and insulting" and used the word to reveal Myrtle's shallow spirit: "'Crazy about him!' cried Myrtle incredulously." In *The Great Gatsby*, Nick "managed to restrain" his "incredulous laughter" but later admitted that his "incredulity was submerged in fascination now."

In his 1940 novel *Native Son*, Richard Wright's Bigger Thomas was "wanting to strike Jan with something because Jan's wide, incredulous stare made him feel hot guilt to the very core of him." Later, "His mother gave him an incredulous stare." Those incredulous stares make one feel something like a wild thing frozen in the headlights.

George Orwell used *incredulous* in *1984*. He wrote that in Big Brother's tyrannical state, it was dangerous "to look incredulous when a victory was announced." In *1984*, "he had no feeling except sheer incredulity," and there was "a sort of incredulous horror that such a word could be applied to himself."

In Arthur Miller's 1953 play *The Crucible*, "He looks at her incredulously," and someone is "pointing at Abigail, incredulously." Of course, when it comes to witch hunts, the world is too credulous, and a touch of incredulity would do it good.

William Golding won a controversial Nobel Prize for literature, largely for his popular young mind's novel *Lord of the Flies*, written in 1954. Golding noted that "They were twins, and the eye was shocked and incredulous at such cheery duplication." In *Lord of the Flies*, we find "Ralph incredulous and faintly indignant." Of course, Ralph is not the only one who is incredulous: "'I can't see no smoke,' said Piggy incredulously." And we read that "Simon, walking in front of Ralph, felt a flicker of incredulity—a beast with claws that scratched, that sat on a mountain-top, that left no tracks."

It is perhaps Joseph Heller's own astonishment that is mirrored in his characters' constant incredulity in his jaded mod-novel *Catch-22*. In *Catch-22*, "he kept repeating to all the bombardiers who inquired incredulously if they were really going to Bologna." And the other characters have their share of incredulity as well: Kid Sampson asks incredulously, General Dreedle roars incredulously, Yossarian cries incredulously, and Milo assails them incredulously at the top of his voice. The word colors the whole novel, as when Yossarian confronts Dobbs: "'Why?' Yossarian stared at Dobbs with an incredulous scowl."

In John Knowles's 1959 two-boy classic *A Separate Peace*, we read, "I turned incredulously, 'You saw Leper?'"

And Nobel Prize-winner Toni Morrison used *incredulous* in *Song of Solomon*. We read, "'You don't know?' Freddie was incredulous," and "'Porter?' The voice was incredulous."

Consider: in literature, characters have incredulous smiles, incredulous stares, and incredulous laughs. They look incredulously at one another, gaze with incredulous curiosity, and betray an ignorant incredulity. There is a slow and incredulous amazement, a look of wonder and incredulity, and an incredulity submerged in fascination.

There are the expectable uses of *incredulous*, as when Fitzgerald described the way "Her host looked at her incredulously." But there are also the surprising and delightful uses of the word, as when Dickens described the French Revolution as the "epoch of incredulity."

Sometimes, a use of *incredulous* is particularly striking, as when Charlotte Brontë described her character "looking darkly and doubtfully on my face, as incredulous of my sanity."

And sometimes, a use of *incredulous* leaves us perplexed and thoughtful, shocked by a quick glimpse of wisdom, as when Melville described the "incredulity which a profound ignorance of the entire subject may induce in some minds."

Perhaps, like an incomprehending dog looking fixedly at a pointing hand, we are missing the...well, the point. Perhaps rather than focus on the fact of our incredulity and the use of our word *incredulous*, we should trace the gaze of our incredulous eyes back to what they see, for it is the chronic incredibility of existence, in all its manifestations, that leaves us incredulous—or that leaves us, as the cool Conrad noted, "overwhelmed by a slow incredulous amazement."

17 tremulous

Our English adjective *tremulous* is a direct descendant of the Latin *tremulus* and the verb *tremere*, to tremble. We call *tremulous* those who are trembling, who are overcome with tremors, or who are overly timid or timorous. If someone is too easily shaken, we might call him tremulous. Tremulous quivering, especially of the hand or voice, might be a result of fear, nervous agitation, or weakness, and it might have either a physical or a psychological origin.

Tremulous has been a popular word among English and American writers for at least three centuries and has been used by Walter Scott, Nathaniel Hawthorne, Lewis Carroll, and Oscar Wilde. Robert Louis Stevenson used it, as did Joseph Conrad and Rudyard Kipling. In modern literature, we find *tremulous* in the works of James Joyce, Richard Wright, Ralph Ellison, George Orwell, and Joseph Heller.

The *Oxford English Dictionary*, which often traces English words back to the thirteenth and fourteenth centuries, finds the first uses of *tremulous* much later, at the beginning of the seventeenth century. Its arrival as a popular English word seems to have come just after Shakespeare's time.

By the early 1800s, *tremulous* was in vogue, and many writers of the nineteenth century used it with relish to describe their trembling, quivering characters. In Mary Shelley's brilliantly imaginative 1816 novel *Frankenstein*, there is a "tremulous and eager hope." In Scott's 1820 *Ivanhoe*, there is "a voice tremulous with passion" and "a voice somewhat tremulous with emotion." James Fenimore Cooper used *tremulous* repeatedly in his woodsy tale *The Last of the Mohicans.* Cooper described "the tremulous glances of his organs, which seemed not to rest a single instant on any particular object." He described "the tremulous voice of Cora." More descriptively, Cooper noted "sounds rendered trebly thrilling by the feeble and tremulous utterance produced by his debility" and observed how the "scout listened to the tremulous voice in which the veteran delivered these words."

Few authors have described the tremblings of humanity as copiously as Nathaniel Hawthorne, who used *tremulous* over and over again in his mid-nineteenth century novels. In *The House of the Seven Gables*, Hawthorne wrote about the "company, tremulous as the leaves of a tree." He described "so tremulous a touch" and heard "a weak, tremulous, wailing voice, indicating helpless alarm." Coolly, Hawthorne observed how at "last, with tremulous limbs, he started up," and he described "Her hand, tremulous with the shrinking purpose which directed it."

In Hawthorne's words, we feel the feeling of *tremulous*, the shaking wailing of helplessness, and the quivering hand of shrinking purpose. Hawthorne had an unusual ability to get inside this word and to understand the interior experiences that cause us to tremble.

In *The Scarlet Letter*, published in 1850, a year before *The House of the Seven Gables*, Hawthorne described tremulous enjoyment, a character "tremulous with the vehemence of his appeal," a "long, deep, and tremulous breath," and "her tremulous gripe." There is "a mouth which, unless when he forcibly compressed it, was apt to be tremulous," and there is "a voice sweet, tremulous, but powerful."

Harriet Beecher Stowe used *tremulous* in *Uncle Tom's Cabin* to describe "the already tremulous state of his nerves."

In *Moby Dick*, Herman Melville noted how "the exhausted mutineer made a tremulous motion of his cramped jaws." Imagine that. Of course, cramped jaws are a condign fate for a mutineer, exhausted or otherwise.

Count on Henry David Thoreau to be different. In his glorious *Walden*, written in 1854 when the dust of civil war was already on the horizon, Thoreau described "a slight tantivy and tremulous motion of the elm tree tops." A tantivy, be it known, is a gallop; the word is also used as an interjection and is uttered as a hunting cry when a chase is at full speed. The tantivy of Thoreau's elm trees, though, was only slight and preceded a tremulous motion.

Charles Dickens used *tremulous* in *A Tale of Two Cities* to describe the horses' "drooping heads and tremulous tails." And George Eliot used it in her *Silas Marner*: "'I'm a worse man than you thought I was, Nancy,' said Godfrey, rather tremulously." In Lewis Carroll's *Alice in Wonderland*, "His voice has a timid and tremulous sound."

No mean wordsmith was Henry James. Writing at the end of the nineteenth century, James had a cosmopolitan, sesquipedalian flair, and he did not shy from using it. In *The American*, James described how "she passed suddenly, as she was very apt to do, from the tone of unsparing persiflage to that of almost tremulous sympathy." In *The American*, "he felt a tremulous impulse to speak out all his trouble." One character is "making at the same time a rapid tremulous movement in the air with his fingers." We read that "Newman's fierce curiosity forced a meaning from the tremulous signs" and that "she wandered off into the dusk with her tremulous taper." Yes, tremulous tapers will do that to you, not to mention unsparing persiflage.

James's *fin de siècle* contemporary, Thomas Hardy, used *tremulous* in *The Return of the Native*, the favorite book Holden Caulfield read at old Pencey. In *The Return of the Native*, she "tremulously inquired," and "she said tremulously." She? Holden's she—Eustacia. One cannot help but wonder what would happen if Eustacia Vye were to meet Holden Caulfield; would they be drawn to each other, or as mutual misfits, would they cancel each other out, finding in each other the qualities they felt to be weakest in themselves? Hardy also used *tremulous* in *The Mayor Casterbridge*, where he described how a character spoke "with eager tremulousness."

In Robert Louis Stevenson's *Treasure Island*, there is a "very tremulous voice," and something is "wavering with the tremulous movement of the water."

Oscar Wilde, whose tragic, Lear-like fall is one of the terrible stories in literary history, used *tremulous* in especially vivid, creative, and memorable ways. In *The Picture of Dorian Gray*, Wilde described "a laburnum, whose tremulous branches seemed hardly able to bear the burden of a beauty so flamelike as theirs." "In the grass," Wilde wrote, "white daisies were tremulous." He observed, horribly, how "the fat manager who met them at the door was beaming from ear to ear with an oily, tremulous smile." And more tolerably, Wilde described how "he remembered her childlike look, and winsome, fanciful ways, and shy, tremulous grace."

In *Kim*, Rudyard Kipling wrote that "In place of the tremulous shrinking trader there lolled against the corner an all but naked, ash-smeared, ochre-barred, dusty-haired Saddhu." Kipling observed how "His lean hand moved tremulously round."

In *Lord Jim*, Joseph Conrad described "a tremulous, subdued, and impassioned note," and in *Heart of Darkness*, he captured the "tremulous and prolonged wail of mournful fear and utter despair." There, now we begin to hear the tone of modern literature. Conrad also described how Marlowe heard Kurtz "say a little tremulously, 'I am lying here in the dark waiting for death.'" And then, the horror, the horror.

For those who do not wish to grow up, there are some literary options, but you have to learn to fly, and you mustn't forget your shadow. In Barrie's *Peter Pan*, where the captain is a Hook and the pirate is a Smee, "John whispered tremulously." We must forgive John this, for even in Never Never Land, he was only a little boy.

In Burnett's *The Secret Garden*, there is a little boy, and there are "two rabbits sitting up and sniffing with tremulous noses." And in this secret garden, characters often speak tremulously.

There is a tremulous whisper in Edith Wharton's *Ethan Frome*.

James Joyce helped to crack open the rigid shells of literary tradition and to free writers for the awesome experiments with language that characterize modern literature. Even in his 1916 *A Portrait of the Artist as a Young Man*, his writing revealed the impulse to break free: "And ecstasy of flight made radiant his eyes and wild his breath and tremulous and wild and radiant his windswept limbs." Joyce described "his tremulous fingers," how a "tremulous chill blew round his heart," and how "His mind was waking slowly to a tremulous morning knowledge, a morning inspiration." Perhaps not everyone wakes to a tremulous morning knowledge, but there can be little doubt that Joyce and Stephen Daedalus, his literary alter ego, did so.

In *As I Lay Dying*, William Faulkner wrote that "Her voice is strong, young, tremulous and clear, rapt with its own timbre and volume."

In *Native Son*, Richard Wright described how "the gleaming metal reflected the tremulous fury of the coals."

One of the most unforgettable scenes in modern literature comes from George Orwell's chilling *1984*, where the slavish populace prostrates itself before Big Brother: "With a tremulous murmur that sounded like 'My Savior!' she extended her arms toward the screen."

In Ralph Ellison's *Invisible Man*, there is "a tremulous, blue-toned chord."

William Golding used *tremulous* in *Lord of the Flies* to describe how "The twins, holding tremulously to each other, dared the few yards to the next shelter and spread the dreadful news." He wrote that "Jack's voice went up, tremulous yet determined, pushing against the uncooperative silence." And it wasn't only Jack who was tremulous: "'I'm chief,' said Ralph tremulously."

Among modern writers, Joseph Heller stands out as a writer who takes full advantage of the range and power of English words. In *Catch-22*, Heller wrote that "the burning plane floated over on its side and began spiraling down slowly in wide, tremulous, narrowing circles."

And so we see that *tremulous*, like other words that have become important in English and American literature, has a full range of uses, from the physical descriptions of tremulous fingers, hands, cramped jaws, limbs, rabbit noses, mouths, horse tails, white daisies, elm leaves, tapers, water, furious coals, and spiraling aircraft; to the analogous quavering of tremulous voices, whispers, wails, blues notes, breath, and murmurs; to the poetic descriptions of tremulous sympathy, a tremulous chill blowing round the heart, and a tremulous morning knowledge.

There is much in life, this word tells us, to make us tremble. We are tremulous with despair, with emotion, and with passion. We are tremulous with the ecstasy of flight. We are tremulous yet determined, tremulous with hope, and tremulous with timidity. We are tremulous when we are eager, and we are tremulous when we are waiting for death.

In *tremulous*, we who speak English have a very human word, a word that shows us at the limits of our courage, at the edge of our confidence, at the circumference of our certainty. We are not, like Homer's Apollo and Athena or Egypt's stone pharaohs, godlike beings who move forward with an absolute knowledge of personal power and assured outcome. We are only human, tremulous with the knowledge of our human limitations and fully aware that the world is at least partially beyond our control, that what we most want may or may not happen. It is this uncertainty that gives our human victories such savor; they are truly victories because the outcome was always in doubt, and our greatest shows of confidence, however brave, are conducted in spite of, not in the absence of, uncertainty.

18visage

The English adjective *visage* has a distinguished ancestry. For us the visage is the face, especially the human face, with emphasis on its visible qualities: its expression, its features, its shape. It is what can be seen. For the ancient Roman troops, whose stern visages looked down from the palisades at barbarian tribes who had a lot of Gaul, *visus* meant face, but it was the participle of *videre*, to see.

Visage is a more formal word than *countenance*, which is a more formal word than *face*. Although both *visage* and *countenance* are used with latitude and are used to describe the face's manifestation of emotions, *countenance* emphasizes the state of mind that the face reveals, while *visage* emphasizes the face's appearance, especially when the face is visibly serious, severe, stern, or angry. And then there is *physiognomy*, which, though it emphasizes the physical features of the face, is also seen as a sign or index of lasting inner character, in contrast to the evanescent feelings that are revealed in the visage and the countenance.

Visage appeared in English literature in the early 1300s, stuck, and has been used by Shakespeare, Milton, Swift, Shelley, Scott, Cooper, the Brontës, Hawthorne, Melville, Dickens, James, Wilde, and Conrad.

By the sixteenth and seventeenth centuries, *visage* had a firm footing in English plays and poems. In Shakespeare's 1596 *Romeo and Juliet*, we find, "Give me a case to put my visage in." In *King Lear*, there is the unforgettable "A plague upon your epileptic visage!" And in *Hamlet*, Shakespeare described "the dejected 'havior of the visage," the "visage of offence," and the "tristful visage." We read that "all his visage wanned, / Tears in his eyes, distraction in 's aspect," and we learn that "We are oft to blame in this— / 'Tis too much proved—that with devotion's visage / And pious action we do sugar o'er / The devil himself."

Milton used *visage* frequently in his 1667 epic poem *Paradise Lost*. He described "Their visages and stature as of Gods," a "Visage drawn," a "visage all intlam'd," "Celestial visages," and "the Anarch old / With falt'ring speech and visage incompos'd." We all, of course, hate to have our visage incompos'd. Milton also described "ire, envy, and despair, / Which marr'd his borrow'd visage, and betray'd / Him counterfeit, if any eye beheld."

In *Gulliver's Travels*, Jonathan Swift observed that "His visage was meager, his hair lank and thin, and his voice hollow" and described how "The ugly monster, when he saw me, distorted several ways every feature of his visage."

In Mary Shelley's 1816 novel *Frankenstein*, the pitiful monster relates how he "travelled only at night, fearful of encountering the visage of a human being," and we learn that "the expression of brutality was wrongly marked in the visage of the second."

Sir Walter Scott used *visage* in his 1820 *Ivanhoe* to describe dark visages with white turbans and to depict the "scars with which his visage was seamed."

One author who loved *visage* and used it copiously was James Fenimore Cooper. In his leafy novel *The Last of the Mohicans*, Cooper described "a human visage, as fiercely wild as savage art and unbridled passions could make it." Cooper wrote that "twenty times he fancied he could distinguish the horrid visages of his lurking foes" and observed "the occasional gleams that shot across his swarthy visage." In *The Last of the Mohicans*, we see "the scowling visage of Chingachgook" and "the dark form and malignant visage of Magua," and we read that "every muscle in his wrinkled visage was working with anguish." There are "inflamed visages" and "swarthy and marked visages," and we find "each dark visage distinctly visible."

In her brooding and heathery *Wuthering Heights*, Emily Brontë wrote, "Seventy times seven times seven didst thou gapingly contort thy visage." Which, of course, is a lot of times.

Emily's sister Charlotte used *visage* in her brave *Jane Eyre*. She observed "thick lineaments in a spacious visage," a bird "hanging its black and scarlet visage over the nest," and a "cicatrised visage." Bird visages, we must suppose, are rarely spacious or cicatrised, and so these two epithets must apply to characters other than the one hanging over the nest. Bird visages would more likely be pinched, vivid, alert, or timid, it seems to us.

Perhaps the author who most relied on *visage* was Nathaniel Hawthorne. In his *The House of the Seven Gables*, he used *visage* repeatedly. We read that "She, in fact, felt a reverence for the pictured visage," that "Her visage is not even ugly," and that "He turned a wrinkled and abominable visage to every passerby." Hawthorne noted that "her visage was growing so perversely stern, and even fierce" and described the "good deal of feeling in his ancient visage." One character is moved "to accuse his own imagination of deluding him with whatever grace had flickered over that visage," and there was a "grim frown on his swarthily white visage." Hawthorne described "a few visages of retired sea captains at the window of an insurance office," a "visage of composed benignity," the "pale visages awaiting her on the landing place above," and the way that "benignity blazes from his visage." Most importantly, Hawthorne used *visage* to describe the face of the house itself; he described "the dilapidated and rusty-visaged House of the Seven Gables" and "the battered visage of the House of the Seven Gables." Not every house, we must aver, can possess such a visage; most, it seems, have conformist visages, timid visages, and diffident visages.

In *The Scarlet Letter*, Hawthorne noticed the "most iron-visaged of the old dames" and "a pale, thin, scholarlike visage." He observed that "his visage was getting sooty with the smoke" and that "a smile...flickered over his visage so derisively."

Hawthorne's friend Herman Melville used *visage* in *Moby Dick*; Melville duly noted that "his swart visage and bold swagger are not unshunned in cities."

In *A Tale of Two Cities*, Charles Dickens described a "rather handsome visage" and a "taciturn and ironbound visage," and in *The American*, jaded Henry James wrote that "Mr. Tristram puckered his plump visage" and that "Mrs. Bread appeared in the background, dim-visaged as usual." More poetically, he described "the comely visage of temptation." If we had to choose among these visages for ourselves and describe our own visages as ironbound, plump, or dim, what would we choose? And what if we added Oscar Wilde's option, from *The Picture of Dorian Gray*: "He was withered, wrinkled, and loathsome of visage"? Can we imagine people describing us in such terms? "Yes, that fellow," they might say, "he is plump, ironbound, and loathsome of visage."

Joseph Conrad described, in his *Heart of Darkness*, this "fair hair, this pale visage, this pure brow," and Joseph Heller, whose heart knew darkness, used *visage* in *Catch-22* to describe "a dark and doleful visage" and "the sheer force of his solemn, domineering visage."

Today, *visage* is less commonly used than in previous literature, but it has not vanished; in Doctorow's *Ragtime*, we find, "I guarantee the visage of the great king will be of considerable interest to you."

All of these *visages* that peer out at us from the pages of English and American literature...what do they tell us? We see visages that are domineering, doleful, pale, and loathsome. Some are plump; some are comely. There are handsome visages, taciturn visages, swart visages, and ancient visages. Some visages are abominable; some are scholarlike, or spacious, or scowling. Some old dames, Hawthorne tells us, are iron-visaged. And some visages are wrinkled, or inflamed, or malignant, or even incomposed.

What did Cooper and Milton mean when they referred to visages as *inflamed*?

What did Charlotte Brontë mean by calling a visage *spacious*?

What did Jonathan Swift mean by calling a visage *meager*?

The visage, it seems, is more often dark than the countenance. Where, in our books, are merry visages, or gay visages, or expectant visages? No, those would be countenances; *visage* is the word we use to communicate the serious, the stern, the unfortunate. We would not describe the mirthful visage of a small child, but such a child could have a mirthful countenance. If the child became lost, her parent could produce a fearful visage, which could give way to a joyful countenance when the child was found.

Life being what it is, we need a goodly handful of such words: *visage, countenance, physiognomy, aspect, mien,* and even *face*, if we are to reflect, in literature, the richness of our lives. Lacking such words as these, one's noble physiognomy would lack a cheerful countenance and would sag under the severity of a disappointed visage.

19 singular

The origin of the English word *singular*, though not simple, is *simple*. That is, the dictionary traces *singular* back to the Latin *singularis* and tells us to look up *single*, which is traced back to the Latin *singulus*, at which point the dictionary tells us to look up *simple*, which traces back to the Latin *simplus/simplex*, at which point the dictionary tells us to look up *simplex*, which turns out be Latin for one-fold, with *sim* meaning one and *plex* meaning fold. Now, maybe *simplex* is not complex to you, but this simple history of *singular* is simplistic, if not simple-minded, since at that point the origin of the word withdraws into the shadows of time and is lost from view.

The meaning of *singular* is about what one would expect: single in nature. Something that is singular can be unique, extraordinary, strange, or exceptional.

This simple word entered the singular English language early; Chaucer wrote of the repentance of "singular synnes" in 1386, two hundred years before Shakespeare used the word in *Romeo and Juliet*.

In English and American literature, *singular* has been used by Milton, Defoe, Swift, Wollstonecraft, Austen, Mary Shelley, Cooper, Thackeray, the Brontës, Hawthorne, Stowe, Melville, George Eliot, Henry James, Hardy, Stevenson, Wilde, Crane, Wells, Kipling, Grahame, Burnett, Wilder, and Knowles.

In these authors' books, we find singular feelings, singular qualifications, singular beauty, and singular expressions. There are singular reasons and singular men, and there are singular discoveries, fortunes, and sounds.

In Shakespeare's *Romeo and Juliet*, we learn that "the jest may remain after the wearing solely singular." Milton described behavior as "singular and rash" in *Paradise Lost*, and Defoe's Robinson Crusoe admitted, concerning Friday, that he "had a singular satisfaction in the fellow himself."

In *Gulliver's Travels*, Jonathan Swift described one character who "took a fancy of diverting himself in a very singular manner," and he reported that Gulliver had "never till then seen a race of mortals so singular in their shapes, habits, and countenances." In fact, their "shape was very singular and deformed." Swift observed "qualifications of so singular a kind" and described "one person whose case appeared a little singular."

In her *Vindication of the Rights of Woman*, Mary Wollstonecraft confessed, "So singular, indeed, are my feelings—and I have endeavoured not to catch factitious ones." Catching factitious (artificial) feelings is certainly a problem, but no one who has read Wollstonecraft's prescient 1792 masterpiece could imagine her as a factitious feeling-catcher.

Jane Austen used *singular* in *Pride and Prejudice*: "'Do you prefer reading to cards?' said he; 'that is rather singular.'" Well, perhaps, but Elizabeth Bennet would. Prefer reading, that is.

Mary Shelley used *singular* frequently in her monster story *Frankenstein*. "During one of their walks," she wrote, "a poor cot in the foldings of a vale attracted their notice, as being singularly disconsolate." In *Frankenstein*, "we found the tree shattered in a singular manner," and there was "a scene of singular beauty." Shelley used *singular* to describe the unique beauty of Germany: "This part of the Rhine, indeed, presents a singularly variegated landscape."

Mary Shelley wrote *Frankenstein* in 1816, ten years before Cooper, on the other side of the Atlantic, wrote *The Last of the Mohicans*. In this novel of forest and fear, Cooper described a "short and silent communication, between two such singular men." He observed "the singular compound of quick, vigilant sagacity and of exquisite simplicity," and he noted how "the young chief took his position with singular caution and undisturbed coolness." In *The Last of the Mohicans*, a warrior's "aim was so singularly and so unexpectedly interrupted," and there was both a "singular indulgence" and a "singular warning."

In *Vanity Fair*, Thackeray wrote that "Now, Miss Amelia Sedley was a young lady of this singular species."

And in Emily Brontë's *Wuthering Heights*, we find "eyes deep set and singular" and "a singular sort of old-fashioned couch, very conveniently designed to obviate the necessity for every member of the family having a room to himself."

Some couch.

In *Jane Eyre*, Emily's sister Charlotte explained that "only singular gleams scintillated in his eyes." This, of course, comes as a relief to everyone tired of common, vulgar gleams.

Hawthorne, who was a contemporary of the Brontë sisters, used *singular* in his novels. In *The House of the Seven Gables*, there was "a singular stir" and a singular tenacity: "they clung to the ancestral house with singular tenacity of home attachment." In *The Scarlet Letter*, there is "a wild and singular appeal," a "singular circumstance," and a "singular expression which he had so often remarked in her black eyes." These things, Hawthorne knew, "may appear singular."

There must have been something in the atmosphere; Thackeray's *Vanity Fair* was published in 1847, the Brontës' *Wuthering Heights* and *Jane Eyre* both came out in 1847, Hawthorne's *The Scarlet Letter* was published in 1850, and 1851 saw the emergence of Stowe's *Uncle Tom's Cabin* and Melville's *Moby Dick*.

Uncle Tom's Cabin has unfortunately given rise to the denigrating epithet *Uncle Tom*, but the book is a heroic attack on the evil and brutality of slavery, and Harriet Beecher Stowe spared no effort to turn readers against the diabolical institution. In *Uncle Tom's Cabin*, she described "some singular reason" and "their singular words and ways." She wrote that there "are things about her so singular" and noted that "Mr. St. Clare is a singular man."

Melville used *singular* in his leviathan tome *Moby Dick* to characterize posture: "I was struck with the singular posture he maintained," and to express wonder: "All this struck me as mighty singular."

George Eliot, who was no average George, wrote about Silas Marner that "his history became blent in a singular manner with the life of his neighbors." That was in 1861, a decade after Melville's *Moby Dick* saw the serene, exasperating light of day.

In 1876 Henry James wrote *The American*. The American in question, Mr. Newman—a name about as subtle as Ebenezer Scrooge—was aware that "a singular feeling took possession of him," and he witnessed a "singular scene."

The hardiest of *singular* users was Thomas Hardy, who wrote in *The Mayor of Casterbridge* of "the most singular news." In *The Return of the Native*, Hardy described something that was "like man, slighted and enduring; and withal singularly colossal and mysterious in its swarthy monotony." Now, what could that be? Hardy wrote that when "he drew nearer he perceived it to be a spring van, ordinary in shape, but singular in colour, this being a lurid red." The driver of the van "carried across his shoulder the singular heart-shaped spade of large dimensions used in that species of labour," and "the grace of his movement was singular." Hardy described how a "sense of novelty in giving audience to that singular figure had been sufficient to draw her forth" and wrote that in one character, "an inner strenuousness was preying upon an outer symmetry, and they rated his look as singular." We hate it when our inner strenuousness preys upon our outer symmetry, do we not? In *The Return of the Native*, "Eustacia looked curiously at the singular man who spoke thus." Hardy wrote that "Nothing in his appearance was at all singular but the fact of its great difference from what he had formerly been." And Hardy captured the ambivalent uncertainty that we feel: "There is an indefinite sense that he must be invading some region of singularity, good or bad."

Robert Louis Stevenson used *singular* in his 1886 *Dr. Jekyll and Mr. Hyde* to describe "a discovery so singular and profound."

And Oscar Wilde used *singular* in his 1890 *The Picture of Dorian Gray* to explain that "the sonorous green jaspers that are found near Cuzco...give forth a note of singular sweetness." Are all jaspers sonorous with notes of singular sweetness, or is it only the green jaspers found near Cuzco?

In *The Red Badge of Courage*, Stephen Crane wrote that "they scampered with singular fortune," and he described how "He and the tattered man began a pursuit. There was a singular race." Crane, of course, wrote his novel in 1895, long after the Civil War had ended but not before the veterans had died; they were incredulous that anyone, let alone someone who had never even been in the war, could have captured it so perfectly on paper.

H.G. Wells's account of *The War of the Worlds* cannot be so easily confirmed, but he did leave a singularly universal description of the war-torn landscape: "The aspect of the place in the dusk was singularly desolate: blackened trees, blackened, desolate ruins."

In Kipling's 1901 *Kim*, "he was explaining to a young man, evidently a neophyte, of singular, though unwashen, beauty." Would a neophyte's beauty be less singular if it were washen, rather than unwashen?

In *The Wind in the Willows*, Kenneth Grahame wrote that "Toad is busily arraying himself in those singularly hideous habiliments so dear to him." Well, Toad would.

In 1911 Frances Hodgson Burnett wrote *The Secret Garden* and described how a "wind was rising and making a singular, wild, low, rushing sound." She observed that "Colin had read about a great many singular things and was somehow a very convincing sort of boy" and that the "singular calmness remained with him the rest of the evening."

Thornton Wilder used *singular* in his 1927 *The Bridge of San Luis Rey* to explain how they "were singularly comforted by his absurd devotion." And John Knowles, in his 1959 *A Separate Peace*, wrote that "the hypnotic power of his voice combined with the singularity of his mind."

Unlike *grotesque, countenance, odious*, and *incredulous, singular* is not a word that makes the peaks of human reaction to the world manifest, but it does reveal our powers of perception; we notice when things are unusual, and we focus when something is weird. Perhaps this is an inbred tendency, born of a thousand millennia of survival conditions. Perhaps it is simply a sign of our lucid intelligence. Either way, we enjoy being able to express, in language, that a mind is a singularity, that a wind has a singular rushing sound, that Toad's habiliments are singularly hideous. We want to indicate that things are not ordinary, that a van is painted a singular color, that someone is somehow adopting a singular posture, and that a man's life is blent in a singular manner with the life of his neighbors. It is not that there is everywhere a singular stir, or that we witness the singular tenacity of home attachment, or that our inner strenuousness preys on our outer symmetry, causing our look to be singular.

No, the commonplaces of life are not singular, they are common, and repetitive, and similar. We become accustomed to them, expect them, and feel comforted that we know how to live with them. And then, when we do not expect it, we come upon something anomalous, something unique, something singular.

20 venerate

To venerate is to revere, to hold in reverence. What is venerated, especially if it is old, is venerable, is an object of veneration. *Venerate* comes from the Latin *veneratus*, the participle of the verb *venerari*, to worship or revere, which traces back eventually to *venus*, loveliness.

Once again, as we speak English, we find that we are speaking Latin, uttering ancient syllables that were once new under a Roman moon, that were sung on Roman ships making night crossings in the Mediterranean, that were spoken by Roman soldiers around campfires in Gaul.

Words, we now know, have an unexpected durability and survive as vital artifacts long after stone cities have crumbled to dust. Once, happy Roman couples strolled through their great city, and the verb *venerari* came lightly to their lips. Two thousand years later, the couples are all gone, their bright city is a vast ancient ruin, and brash tourists from a two-century-recent nation across the Atlantic walk the surface of the buried past and unknowingly use the word *venerate*.

The language of the tourists, English, did not exist during the Roman Empire and would not exist for more than a thousand years. Eventually, history would sweep together the remains of Latin, Greek, German, and sundry other tongues to form a new, unkempt, and ill-disciplined hodgepodge of words and syntaxes that would become the impure but potent crudity known as the English language. Like American society, English draws its power from its diversity; in response to any of life's absurdities, English can draw upon a multifarious orchestra of vowels and consonants that more sensible languages cannot match. English is the mockingbird of modern languages. Today, English expresses the idea of reverence by echoing the Roman *veneratus*: *venerate* is how we put it—how we have put it, actually, for centuries. In 1719, twenty-four years before Thomas Jefferson was born, Defoe used it in *Robinson Crusoe* to describe "the veneration of the people to the clergy."

In 1726 Jonathan Swift used *venerate* in *Gulliver's Travels* with ironic force to describe "the Judges, those venerable sages and interpreters of the law." Through the gullible mouth of his protagonist, Swift described "every quality which procures veneration, love, and esteem" and observed that "a constellation of virtues in such amiable persons produced in me the highest veneration." Swift also noted that "I have too great a veneration for crowned heads" and wrote that "I was struck with a profound veneration at the sight of Brutus."

Mary Wollstonecraft, who did not venerate lightly, wrote in her *Vindication of the Rights of Woman* that "moss-covered opinions assume the disproportioned form of prejudices when they are indolently adopted only because age has given them a venerable aspect"—a brilliant sentence that stirs the admiration of any reader whose brain is not indolent. Wollstonecraft also described the "venerable aspect of a duty" and observed that men "venerate the right of possession, as a stronghold." Such words excite controversy and resentment even today. In every generation there is some sturdy individual whose eyes seem focused four centuries forward; it is a wonder that, writing twentieth-century ideas in 1792, Wollstonecraft was not hanged.

In *Pride and Prejudice*, published three decades before the Brontë sisters came to print, the pioneering Jane Austen imagined the odious Mr. Collins, who was enraptured by the condescending patronage of Lady Catherine de Bourgh; Austen noted "his veneration for her as his patroness."

In Mary Shelley's *Frankenstein*, there is a "Beloved and venerable parent," as well as the observation that "Nothing could exceed the love and respect which the younger cottagers exhibited towards their venerable companion."

The Saxon Gurth, in Sir Walter Scott's 1820 *Ivanhoe*, kisses a noble hand "with the utmost possible veneration."

James Fenimore Cooper used *venerate* in *The Last of the Mohicans*. Cooper wrote that the "high northwest Indians, not having as yet got the traders among them, continue to venerate the beaver" and that "the venerable father took a part in the interrogatories, with an interest too imposing to be denied." In Cooper's green saga, a character "opened the volume with a care and veneration suited to its sacred purposes"; another character "paused, and looked about him, in affected veneration for the departed," and a third looked "in his face with the fondness and veneration of a favored child."

In *Vanity Fair*, Thackeray described how "an autograph letter of her sister, Miss Pinkerton, was an object of as deep veneration as would have been a letter from a sovereign."

Vanity Fair was published in 1847, the same year that Charlotte Brontë published *Jane Eyre*, the character by which name noted, "I have a considerable organ of veneration," and later added, "I deeply venerated my cousin's talent and principle."

Writing at the midpoint of the nineteenth century, Nathaniel Hawthorne loved *venerate*, especially in its adjective transformation *venerable*. In *The House of the Seven Gables*, he wrote that "The aspect of the venerable mansion has always affected me like a human countenance." Hawthorne described "venerable beards" and the "venerable house itself" and noted that the "venerable man made pretensions to no little wisdom." Unexpectedly, Hawthorne applied *venerable* to a chicken, which was "almost as venerable in appearance as its mother." Lucky chicken, for then, "She called Chanticleer, his two wives and the venerable chicken, and threw them some crumbs of bread from the breakfast table." Cooper also observed "that graybearded and wrinkled profligate, decrepit without being venerable—as a tender stripling, capable of being improved into all that it ought to be." Pushing the limits of viable vocabulary, Cooper wrote, "What a treasure trove to these venerable quidnuncs, could they have guessed the secret which Hepzibah and Clifford were carrying along with them!" Now, gentle reader, know that a quidnunc, from the Latin *what now?*, is a gossip.

In *The Scarlet Letter*, Hawthorne turned his gaze upon Puritan New England, where "the severest acts of public discipline were alike made venerable and awful." Hawthorne described "a venerable minister or magistrate," "a venerable pastor," and even "the venerable structure of King's Chapel." For Reverend Dimmesdale, who was venerated by his public, no one knew "the agony with which this public veneration tortured him."

The year 1851 saw the publication of *The House of the Seven Gables*, *Uncle Tom's Cabin*, and *Moby Dick*. Perhaps the weight of the times is reflected in the magnitude of the literature. In *Uncle Tom's Cabin*, Harriet Beecher Stowe created a character "gazing upward with a face fervent with veneration."

In Melville's *Moby Dick*, we find "a man of a certain venerable robustness," and we read a poetic description of a ship: "Her venerable bows looked bearded." Melville described types of whales: "In one respect this is the most venerable of the leviathans, being the one first regularly hunted by man," and he described the leviathan as having a "vast and venerable head."

In Thoreau's *Walden*, published in 1854, we find "a venerable moss-grown and hoary ruin."

In Dickens's *A Tale of Two Cities*, there are "venerable and feeble persons."

George Eliot used *venerable* in her sad story *Silas Marner* to describe "the prescriptive respectability of a family with a mural monument and venerable tankards." Right: when it comes to status symbols, those venerable tankards do it every time—really gets the quidnuncs going. Eliot also described "a venerable and unique parlour, which was the extremity of grandeur in her experience."

In Henry James's *The American*, there is a "venerable friend," a "certain venerable rosiness in her cheek," and a promise "to treat the young girl with nothing less than veneration."

It is difficult to think of the diffident and urbane Henry James and the humorous and colloquial Mark Twain as contemporaries, but they were. *The American* and *Tom Sawyer*, about as different as two American novels could be, were both published in 1876. While James was describing a cheek's venerable rosiness, Twain was aiming his wink at "the bent and venerable Major and Mrs. Ward."

Thomas Hardy, who quit writing good novels when the critics would not quit writing bad things about them, used *venerable* in all of his books and undoubtedly would have used it in the future books that remained unwritten. In *The Mayor of Casterbridge*, Hardy described "All the venerable contrivances and confusions which delighted the eye by their quaintness." He described "the venerable town" and observed farming practices near Casterbridge, "where the venerable seed-lip was still used for sowing as in the days of the Heptarchy."

In his 1900 novel *Lord Jim*, Joseph Conrad described "the venerable gray hairs of his pigtail," and in his 1902 *Heart of Darkness*, he wrote, "We looked at the venerable stream not in the vivid flush of a short day."

In Kipling's 1901 *Kim*, "the lama was a great and venerable curiosity."

Thornton Wilder used *veneration* in his 1927 novel *The Bridge of San Luis Rey*. Wilder noted "the veneration for great poets" and wrote that "at least they never submitted to the boredom of a misplaced veneration."

In Orwell's chilling *1984*, written in 1949, he described Winston Smith's ultimate defeat, the loss of his individuality to the power of the mechanistic, totalitarian state: in the end, Winston betrayed his love Julia, and "he venerated Big Brother."

John Knowles described a "venerable, entrenched institution" in *A Separate Peace*.

That was in 1959. The next year, Harper Lee used *venerable* in *To Kill a Mockingbird*. "The Maycomb jail," she wrote, "was the most venerable of the county's buildings."

We see, in literature, a picture of the many things we venerate: old buildings, crowned heads, and the right of possession, beards, bows, and severe acts of public discipline. We venerate feeble persons, bent persons, and quidnuncs. We venerate parents, and moss-covered opinions, and pastors, ministers, and chapels. There are venerable gray hairs on pigtails, and venerable poets, and venerable books.

Sometimes, veneration goes wrong. Sometimes we submit to the boredom of a misplaced veneration, and sometimes age gives a venerable aspect to an indolently adopted prejudice. Sometimes there is an affected veneration for the departed.

But sometimes veneration goes right, and we treat a young girl with nothing less than veneration. Sometimes we greet a venerable friend. Sometimes our faces are fervent with veneration when we see a constellation of virtues in amiable people.

It is interesting that, in all of these works, there is no trace of self-veneration. Veneration, it seems, can never be egocentric or narcissistic; it is a one-way process. It is outward. Like time, it moves in one direction only, though no one can say why. Veneration flows out from ourselves, leads us beyond ourselves, and turns our minds to the admiration of someone or something else, to an outward dignity that we regard as worthy of our sincerest respect.

Of course, our sense of irony sometimes comes into play. Held in veneration are Orwell's Brother, Melville's leviathan, and Hawthorne's chicken, not to mention Kipling's lama, Conrad's gray hairs, Swift's crowned heads, Knowles's entrenched institution, and Eliot's tankards.

Those, however, are only ironies. True veneration is simple and sincere. The estimable Jane Eyre said that she had a considerable organ of veneration—surely a good thing to have. And Cooper described the fondness and veneration of a favored child. For Defoe, veneration was "profound"; for Charlotte Brontë, it was deep.

The salient presence of this word in English and American literature gives us yet another insight into the goodness of our own natures; what would it mean if our literature did not promote this word, or—worse—if our language did not contain this word? Would we want to live in a society that did not know veneration, that did not find venerable what is old, enduring, surviving? Would we want to live in a society devoid of reverence, of individuals caring for things beyond themselves? What, before we turn our attention to something else, is the antonym of *venerate*?

21 conclusion

The classic words in this book—*countenance, profound, manifest, serene, sublime, prodigious, acute, clamor, exquisite, languor, grotesque, condescend, allude, odious, placid, incredulous, tremulous, visage, singular,* and *venerate*—form a kind of microepic of all humanity. They are central. They bring to a distilled essence the feelings and reactions that form the fabric of our spirit. They have a universality that transcends any location, and they could just as easily describe *The Iliad* as they could describe the Battle of Shiloh or an opera by Mozart.

If we imagine applying these classic words to any situation, we can see why they have such prominence in English and American literature. To turn the idea the other way around, just imagine a situation to which none of these words would apply; it would have to be something pallid and objective, like the instructions for assembling a machine.

But human lives and aspirations are not mechanical objects. They are sublime and exquisite. On our countenances are written our feelings of incredulity in the face of the grotesque, our prodigious imaginations, our acute fears and dreams. We recoil from the odious, and we retreat to the serene and placid.

These and other essential words in our language have stood the test of time. For more than four centuries, they have been the tough fibers that the best writers have woven for significance and descriptive power. From Shakespeare to the Brontës, from Melville to Sylvia Plath, English and American writers have seen the human spirit in *countenance*, *grotesque*, *serene*, and *sublime*.

The mainstays of classic books, these are classic words, whose worth is manifest. Carl Sandburg once said, "Ya gotta write a poem one word at a time." That being so, for poems and all other writing, it is well if each word is good.

These words are good.

22 100 classic words

The classic words discussed in this book are a worthy collection whose presence in English and American literature is manifestly strong and important. They offer proof, if proof is needed, that the direct study of vocabulary is both valid and exciting and that the words one learns not only reappear in further reading but also help the life of the mind to be richer and more satisfying. For anyone who would like a list of the top 100 words in the Classic Words database, in descending order, here it is:

1. countenance
2. profound
3. serene
4. manifest
5. languor
6. acute
7. prodigious
8. grotesque
9. sublime
10. allude
11. exquisite
12. condescend
13. clamor
14. singular
15. placid
16. incredulous
17. tremulous
18. odious
19. visage
20. venerate
21. amiable
22. vivid
23. sagacity
24. vulgar
25. melancholy
26. abate
27. undulate
28. traverse
29. repose
30. wistful
31. palpable
32. pallor
33. superfluous
34. perplex
35. lurid
36. furtive
37. subtle
38. articulate
39. remonstrate
40. stolid
41. audible
42. somber
43. prostrate
44. vex
45. abyss
46. pervade
47. sallow
48. genial
49. portent
50. torpid

51. abject	76. imperious
52. austere	77. derision
53. rebuke	78. profuse
54. dejection	79. apprehension
55. vivacious	80. martyr
56. despond	81. billow
57. importune	82. droll
58. oblique	83. resolute
59. pensive	84. alacrity
60. impend	85. phenomenon
61. peremptory	86. reproof
62. doleful	87. affect
63. aloof	88. listless
64. tedious	89. wan
65. tangible	90. morose
66. magnanimous	91. physiognomy
67. indolent	92. dissipate
68. retort	93. ignominy
69. inexorable	94. malevolence
70. benevolence	95. abash
71. procure	96. felicity
72. expostulate	97. jovial
73. ostentatious	98. affable
74. obsequious	99. oppress
75. eccentric	100. fain